Legacy of the Lotus

(The Friend's Quest 2)

Harshitha Hebbar

Darpan

An Imprint of Prism Books Pvt. Ltd

Legacy of the Lotus

(The Friend's Quest 2)

Published by

Darpan – An Imprint of Prism Books Pvt. Ltd.

1865, 32nd Cross, 10th Main, BSK II Stage, Bengaluru -560 070
Phone: 080-26714108, Telefax : 080-26713979
e-mail : info@prismbooks.com | Website: www.prismbooks.com

Also at:

Chennai : 044-24311244, prismchennai@prismbooks.com
Hyderabad : 040-27612938, prismhyderabad@prismbooks.com
Kochi : 0484-4000945, prismkochi@prismbooks.com
Kolkata : 033-24297957, prismkolkata@prismbooks.com

Pages : 108
ISBN 10 : 93-86506 -07-6
ISBN 13 : 978-93-86506-07-8
Price : ₹125
Layout &
Cover design : enablePrint, Bengaluru

Dedicated to
my family and friends

Note from the Author

First and foremost, I thank my family for supporting and helping me. Special thanks to my mother for encouraging me through the writer's block I faced. A big thank you to Mrs. Sowbhagya Eswaraiah for the wonderful foreword. It means a lot to me.

My sincere thanks goes to Prism Books Pvt. Ltd for publishing my book. I would also like to thank my friends and teachers for encouraging me. Above all, thank you readers!

Reach me at: harshithahebbar23@gmail.com

Harshitha Hebbar

Foreword

> The role of a writer is not to say what we can all say, but what we are unable to say.
>
> —Anais Nin

It is said that it is never too late to start anything in life. But this young author, who is studying in 8th standard has redefined that statement and has started writing from a young age. Well, she is still very young !

For me what stood out in the book *Legacy of the Lotus* (The Friend's Quest 2) is the clarity of the thought of the young author which is a refreshing change. She is sure what she wants to say and has narrated the story with remarkable ease and simplicity. Also, the attention to detail for each character cannot be missed!

The book talks about the adventures of the characters Ron, Pal, Amy, Max etc. and their incredible adventure in the Southern part of India. It has a few life lessons as well - never underestimate your enemy !

The book is a must read - especially for children as it talks about the challenges that they will face in their lives and how to overcome them .

Harshitha, take a bow. You have a bright future ahead !

My love and blessings to this young talented writer. The world is an oyster and you are its pearl.

Sowbhagya Eswaraiah
Principal(Rtd)
Government Polytechnic College for Women
Bangalore

March 25, 2017

CHARACTERS

Ron	Formerly from Earth, now a Ronen
Pal	Golden Retriever, Ron’s bond
Carra	Formerly from Earth, now a Ronen
Tabitha	Persian Cat, Carra’s bond
May	Formerly from Earth, now a Ronen
Snowflake	White rabbit, May’s bond
Josh	Formerly from Earth, now a Ronen
Pete	Parrot, Josh’s bond
Amy	Carra’s mother
Max	Ron’s father
Lyke	Streo
Zevyn	Streo, Lyke’s sister
Avaron	Leader of the Ronens
Chester	Lion, Avaron’s bond
Iris	Ronen, daughter of Avaron
Ruben	Hawk, Iris’ bond
Ivy	Ronen, daughter of Avaron
Victoria	White tiger, Ivy’s bond
Leif	Ronen, Avaron’s son
Romial	Ronen deputy
Miva	Leader of the Streos

Chapter 1

Ron dashed along the sandy track, trying to overtake his speedy friend Josh. An idea formed in his mind, and the boy transformed into a cheetah. He overtook Josh and crossed the finish line first. He sat there, very tired.

"Cheating! Cheating!" Josh panted as he crossed the line. The cheetah shrugged and changed back into Ron.

The four friends May, Carra, Ron and Josh were in Imagneus, a planet far from Earth. The four had been normal Earthlings until they met Iris, a Ronen, and joined her race as Ronens, and had all travelled to Imagneus. It was tough though, as their parents agreed to send them with only one parent for each. The Ronens were preparing for a war in Imagneus against an evil Streo called Grinlaut. They won over Grinlaut, and had spent the past two months rebuilding their homeland.

"That is not cheating," Avaron, the leader and Iris' father, said.

"How come?" Josh asked, surprised.

"It is part of Ronen to transform. That trait will, of course, be allowed in every competition."

"But it didn't say so in the banner!" Josh protested.

"That goes without saying," Avaron smiled.

The four friends had been transformed into Ronens, and the Clan had accepted them readily.

Ron was ecstatic. He punched Josh, who wasn't ready to accept that he had lost a running race for the first time ever in his life.

Ron grinned and looked up. Satiro, one of the three moons on Imagneus, was out. Quirodon was partly visible, half hidden by clouds. The other came and went as it pleased. There was no telling that Faztex would rise. Faztex was the auspicious blue moon, Quirodon was the lucky silver moon and Satiro was the beautiful red moon. Each moon had its own night- Dusk of Satiro, Dawn of Quirodon, and the Night of Faztex.

Josh sighed wearily and trudged past other celebrating Ronens to his makeshift bed.

The Ronens always held ceremonies, functions and parties only on the nights when Faztex rose. They did so because it was said that the Ronens rose to glory from ashes on the Night of Faztex. Ivy and Leif, Iris' siblings had told the four the story-

"The leader then was Kortis. He was selected as the leader, and everyone had high hopes; he was young, strong and had a lot of ambition. He strengthened the clan and was a just and kind leader. He was the one who started the tradition of worshipping the moons. He took back the lands that had been stolen from them. One night, he decided to defeat the tyrant king of Imagneus, and he led the Ronens along with other clans to battle on the Night of Faztex. We won, and Kortis himself was chosen as the king of Imagneus. Now the tradition of kings is gone, but still we celebrate the Night of Faztex."

Ron reached the bedroom first, and fell on his bed happily. The camp was not yet fully restored, and everyone had to make-do with what they had. Pal, Ron's bond, climbed onto Ron's bed and squashed him under his weight. Ron shoved the dog off, and Pal whimpered. Josh made his grand entry and slumped on his bed. Carra and May came in, called out a 'good night' and the four were sleeping by the time their parents came in.

They woke up to Victoria's morning alarm. Tabitha, Carra's bond, a cat, mewed a greeting and strolled out, with Carra beside her, with Ron and Pal following. May waved to them from where she and her bond were helping May's mother to cook. Josh was left in his bed, sleeping.

The friends joined Iris and her sisters at the table, where the Ronens were serving breakfast. Ruben, a magnificent hawk, also Iris' bond, flew over and sat down beside them.

"Where is Josh?" Ivy asked.

"Snoring," Tabitha mewed, yawning.

"She asked 'where is he', not 'what's he doing'," Ron pointed out.

"He's snoring in Jupiter. Happy?" Tabitha twitched her tail, irritated.

When they were washing the plates after breakfast, Josh dashed over. "What'd I miss?" He panted.

"Most important meal of the day," May said. "There's some left I think. Go eat quickly." He raced off, leaving clouds of dust trailing behind him.

The four met later on, with Iris, and decided to go for a walk. No sooner had they set foot out of the camp, that they heard Romial, the deputy, call May and Ron. The two quickly muttered their farewell and ran away with their bonds.

Iris, Carra and Josh strolled around the camp, wondering what to do, when suddenly, a horrifying screech caused them to look up. A three-legged beast with a monstrous face and short wings was hovering in the air, clutching a young boy, who was wailing desperately. He had white feathery wings, which were cruelly tied up. The creature let go of the boy, and he fell straight amidst the massing Ronens.

❋ ❋ ❋

The plan would work perfectly. The Shadow of Death watched the events unfold on his magical waterfall with unpleasant happiness. The shimmering water on the waterfall showed his trusted captain, Gillsor, dropping the winged boy into the Ronen Clan. He let out an evil chuckle. He watched with avid interest as an eagle (or was it a hawk?) grab the boy and lay him gently on the ground. The scarred face of the Shadow twisted into a hideous smile. His animal-like yellow eyes glittered hungrily, desiring a power only the Ronens could hand him.

* * *

The winged boy was waking up. He groaned, then bolted up straight, fully alert. Two score Ronens stood watching him suspiciously. Three Ronens were standing near his bed. One was gazing at him curiously, inspecting his hand, which was mysteriously glowing faintly. The boy pulled his hand away. The other two were checking a list and muttering something.

"Herbulen, step aside," a tall man strode forward, gently shoving the doctor aside. "What's your name?" He asked.

"Fivlon," the boy said. "Harra boschon," the boy said. He muttered something else inaudible, and his eyes welled up with tears. He furled and unfurled his wings, and then let it lay limp at his sides.

The tall man looked at him, and then said, "Leave him for now. Apparently, he doesn't know English."

He posted two guards outside the room, and left with the others. The boy looked at the closed door, and smiled cunningly. How easy it was to fool them! Of course he knew the language! Why, hadn't he been the one to endure years of suffering by following them to Earth and noting their every move? *No time to waste*, he thought, and pulled out a small disk from his wings. His wings were the latest edition which came with extra large storage.

There were a number of dials on the disk. He pressed them in a pattern, and it started turning slowly. It clicked once, twice, and then a beam of light fell on it. It turned faster and faster, enlarging as it spun, until it was the size of a basket. Then it stopped, and the light flickered and was gone. The disk glowed with the same light his hand had glowed with. The Shadow of Death's face appeared, cruel and menacing as usual. The Shadow smiled, and the boy knew the Death Lord was pleased with him.

Chapter 2

Iris, Ron, May and Ruben had gone for a stroll in the forest when they were joined by Lykenzar. Lykenzar was a Streo, son of the evil Grinlaut. Lyke's mother had killed Grinlaut. Now his mother, his sister Zevyn and he were staying with the Ronens.

"Who is that boy?" he asked.

"Dunno," Ron shrugged. "He blabbered some gibberish when he got here."

"Hmm," Lykenzar furrowed his eyebrows, lost in thought. "Do you know the Shadow?" he asked suddenly.

"Shadow? Are you referring to this?" Ron asked, pointing to his shadow.

"No, no. The Shadow of Death, Shadow, Death Lord. Have you ever heard of him?"

"No," Ruben said, puzzled.

Lyke just nodded. "Are you going to tell us who he is?" May asked.

"He's dangerous. Beware the boy. He's an accomplice of the Shadow," Lyke said and disappeared into the undergrowth, his brown wolf tail twitching.

Ron looked at May and Iris. The two shrugged, and they resumed their walk.

Lyke was talking to his sister, Zevyn, when the three, with Ruben, returned from their walk. The two were arguing heatedly.

"So? Does it very much matter? Yes, he is trouble, his

character spells that out, but do you really think that running off on a foolhardy mission will solve him?" Zevyn was asking her brother.

"It is most likely that he will cause problems quicker than you can say 'Ronen'. Ivy's parents might see through his veil someday, but what if it's too late then? I'm sure..." Lyke broke off when he saw the three standing there.

"You know what guys? I'm just going to go catch up on my sleep. You guys can continue," Ron started slowly backing away. "You are not going anywhere." Iris grabbed his jacket and pulled him back to the ragged circle they had formed.

"We need to find out that boy's intention. He means no good, I can smell trouble," Zevyn said, flicking her catlike ears. Her eyes turned huge as Ron suddenly tumbled down, face on the floor.

"Score!" Pal cheered from on top of Ron's back. "Pal!" Ron screeched. The golden retriever jumped off his bond's back and sat on the ground. Ron got up painfully, helped by Lyke. As Ron nursed his back, Lyke gently scolded Pal. Lyke never went hard on canines, because he too was part dog. But Zevyn was more cat, and had an attachment to felines.

"Lyke," Zevyn tapped the ground impatiently. He got up, and they continued their discussion, this time joined by Pal and Snowflake, who had appeared to see Pal's 'score'.

"You are right, Zevyn. We do have to find out what exactly that boy is up to." Lyke agreed. "What should we do?" Snowflake asked quietly.

"Start off by telling your parents that he works for the Shadow. They know who he is," Zevyn addressed Iris. "And they will know of his deeds as well," she muttered too soft so that the others won't hear. Iris nodded.

"But how will they know who this Shadow guy is?" Ron asked indignantly. "They will, trust me," Lyke said.

"Come on, then. What are you waiting for?" May said, setting off.

Iris smiled as she followed her cheerful friend. They were joined by Josh, Carra and Ivy, who saw them walking by.

"What's going on?" Pete, Josh's bond, asked.

"You will get to know soon," Zevyn muttered darkly, twitching her ears in fear and anxiety. Ivy and Carra exchanged glances. The winged girl was short tempered, but never this grumpy. They followed Iris into the leader's cabin.

"Mother, Father? Can we come in?" Iris called out. "Come in!" her mother called cheerfully from inside. The group trudged in.

"What is it?" Avaron, the leader asked. "It's about the new boy," Lyke mumbled. He seemed to be uncomfortable talking about the boy.

"Well? What about him?" Iris' mother narrowed her sharp green eyes curiously.

"We know him," Zevyn stepped forward confidently. "He works for the Death Lord." The two leaders let out gasps.

"What?"

A sharp roar made them turn around. Chester, Avaron's bond, and Raptor, the leader's wife's bond, stood side by side at the door.

"Impossible," Raptor muttered, shaking his black head. The two lions entered and sat beside their bonds. "It's true!" Zevyn insisted.

"That explains why there was a weird sound from his room last night," Avaron murmured.

"What does he want?" Josh asked.

Avaron looked up. He started telling a story. As he spoke, his eyes glazed over, as if drowning in the memory.

"The Shadow of Death always wanted power. He bears scars of the battles he fought and won in search of power. He massacred my earlier tribe. You do know that I was not always Ronen, don't you?" He asked, looking up.

"Well, yeah. But they told us that you got lost and found the Ronens," Carra said, pointing at Ivy and Iris.

"That is because I told them that. I had not got lost; my mother took me to the Ronens and begged them to keep me. She did not survive though. Shortly after the Ronens took us in, she died of her injuries. The Shadow had done that to our tribe. So, I grew up here. When I was young, I dreamed of vengeance. But the leader told me revenge is not always the answer. He looked after me like a father. My dreams of revenge faded away, and instead, I became leader. But now that he has come back, I think my chance has come," he ended with a sigh. "But I'm getting old. I do not think I can do it."

The friends listened in silence.

"But what is he after?" Tabitha asked finally. Everyone looked at the white cat. "He is after something, isn't he?"

"Yes. Someone please fetch Minkin." There was a scrabbling sound as Josh and Ron both rushed to the entrance. Josh beat Ron to the entrance and dashed out. He raced in after some time, with Minkin walking at his own pace.

"What did you want, Avaron?" Minkin asked, stepping in. Avaron repeated the incidents. "What do you think he is after?" he asked.

"Hmm. Do you think he is after the treasure?" Minkin mused thoughtfully.

"What treasure?" Snowflake asked.

"The grand treasure of the Ronens. It is a lotus, a white, glittering lotus made of diamonds. It lies in an unexplored, dangerous part of Earth. It is the key to a secret which only the leader of the Clan knows. The Shadow must be after it," Avaron said.

"Why is it on Earth?" Ron asked. Carra rolled her eyes. May stared at him in exasperation. Ron looked around. "Why is it on Earth?" he repeated stupidly.

"The Ronens had sent someone to hide it away in a dangerous place. Later we got to know it was on Earth. And now the Shadow is after it," he let out a sigh. "I need that lotus now. It is the only way to defeat the Shadow of Death."

He looked up. Everyone was watching him in silence. The children had different looks on their faces. Lykenzar and Josh looked determined to get the lotus. Ron looked frightened. Zevyn was smiling; the thought of adventure tempted her. Carra was surprised at the news. May had narrowed her eyes, clouded with thoughts. Iris and Ivy were looking at him with keen interest. The animals, though, seemed only willing to do whatever their bonds wanted to do.

"Where exactly is it?" Josh asked.

"It's not in the ocean, is it?" Ron asked. Ever since their last escapade over the ocean, Ron had been petrified of oceans.

"No," Avaron chuckled. "It's in the middle of a very dangerous forest. Don't look so excited, there is absolutely no way I am sending you children there."

"It is a very dangerous place, as he said. It is certainly not a place for children like you. There are mythical creatures guarding the lotus, ones you have never encountered or seen the likes of before," Iris' mother warned sternly. Lykenzar looked disappointed.

"Then how will you get it back?" Josh asked.

"I will send a strong team to retrieve it for me," The clan leader said. "Chester, can you get Romial for me? I want to discuss this with him."

Chester and Raptor went together. The two had grown very close, and did almost everything together.

The friends also exited the cave. Instantly Ivy was called away for some work. She was very busy now that she was counted an adult in the clan.

Lykenzar still looked determined to go. Two days later, he elaborated a plan of sneaking into the retrieval party and staying hidden until they reached Earth. "They will not be able to do anything then," he said proudly.

Pete screeched with laughter. Lyke glared at him. "You can't pull off something like that," the parrot said. "I am not stupid, you know," Lyke muttered. "Avaron will find out, no matter how clever you try to act," Tabitha said, shaking her head.

Ruben agreed. Victoria suddenly whipped her head around, in the direction of the forest. Ruben and Pete immediately spread their wings and took to the skies. Iris looked up worriedly.

The two birds landed.

"What's up?" Pal asked. "There's something wrong," Ruben said.

"No time to explain?" Tabitha asked sarcastically. "Tell Avaron," Zevyn replied. They turned to go, but Josh had already disappeared. He emerged out of the leader's cave a few seconds later, with Avaron at his side.

There was a lot of noise as the winged army rose to the sky and positioned themselves, ready for attack from the air. A scout immediately swooped forward, unseen by any rival. She came back safely.

"It's the Death Lord," she said, her green eyes visibly worried. "Great Stars, have mercy on us!" Iris' mother cried.

"The retrieval party hasn't left yet. It's impossible to send them now! We need them on the army. What do we do now?" Avaron desperately turned to his wife for advice.

"There's nothing else to do," she said flatly. "Send the children."

Chapter 3

Both Avaron and Lyke's eyes widened, but for different reasons. The leader was shocked and stared at his wife in disbelief; Lyke was overjoyed and surprised.

"But we cannot!" Avaron exclaimed.

"Would you rather have the entire clan massacred or let the children go on a mission they can accomplish?" Iris' mother countered. Lyke nodded vigorously, whispering, "You have my full support."

"Very well. You may go, but not you, Ivy, nor you, Victoria. We need both of your support here. You can send your wishes to your sister, but you have to stay here," Avaron shook his head. Ivy opened her mouth to argue, but then decided not to.

Instead, she and Victoria turned to their friends.They quickly said their farewells, and stood aside. Avaron approached them. Lyke and his sister were quivering with excitement.

"Take Minkin with you to the edge of the forest. He will know what to do. Take care, and all the best. May good luck go with you," he said quickly, ushering them to the edge of the clearing.

Minkin joined them shortly, and the group swiftly made their way to the border of the forest. Minkin looked up at the sky. It was full of dark heavy clouds. He looked back at the little band of animals and Ronens.

He quickly arranged a few vials of coloured mist, which formed shapes of each of the beings present there. Snowflake sniffed it tentatively. It immediately formed a very ghastly look alike of her. She shuddered and retreated to the group. Minkin smiled.

"Do not take any notice of them. They like to scare others a lot," he explained. He set a few other glass bottles around it with the help of his bond, who had accompanied them. He started mumbling a series of spells. Thunder rumbled overhead, and a flash of lightning blinded everyone momentarily.

When they opened their eyes again, they saw the clouds opening up, leaving a small gap between them. A yellow light flooded through the opening and formed a circle a few feet in front of them.

"When you step in that circle you will be transported back to Earth. But before you go, we have to change Lykenzar and Zevyn into normal human beings. It will take only a momentum or two," Minkin took a phial of blue mist and, muttering another string of indistinguishable spells, opened the phial and let it engulf the two siblings.

When the mist cleared, Lykenzar had lost his paws and tail. Zevyn didn't have her wings, and her ears were humanlike now.

Immediately, Minkin pushed all of them into the spot of light, which seemed to be dancing in impatience.

Iris and Pal, who were at the head of the group, floated upwards upon entering the shaft of light. The others were only a footstep behind. They reached the source of the light, and disappeared all at once. Minkin, watching their progress, nodded in satisfaction and hurried back to camp with his bond at his side.

* * *

"I can't believe he did that!" Zevyn complained.

"Look at this! Just *look* at it! This is so amazing!" Unlike his sister, Lykenzar was enjoying every little insect, every single leaf, every shaft of the sunlight in the woods they had emerged in.

Ruben had floated upwards on the thermal currents, and was soaring around. He met a fellow hawk, and was gliding with him. Pete preferred to ride on Josh's shoulder, occasionally roosting on Pal's back. Tabitha and Snowflake padded side by side, behind Zevyn. May and Iris were leading the group, searching for fresh water. They still didn't know where they had emerged, but Carra reckoned it was somewhere in the Caledonian forest in Scotland.

"I'd been here once before," she said.

They walked on, passing a curious woodpecker who decided to follow them all the way. They came to the borderline. Carra pushed her way to the front, blinking in the sunlight. Her eyes widened when she saw a hauntingly familiar figure.

She dashed away from the cover of the trees, nearly colliding with the figure.

"Mom! It's me, Carra!" she cried. Her mother, Amy, let out an 'oh! in shock. Recognition broke out on her face like sunlight, and she instantly hugged her daughter.

"I missed you so much, sweetie," her mother whispered. She held her daughter by her shoulders and pushed her away, squinting at her. "Let's have a good look at you," she said, scrutinizing Carra. "Hmmm, you look just the same."

The others emerged from the woods. Amy looked up in surprise. "Ron! May, Josh!" she called out happily. She looked at the other children in bewilderment. "Who are those kids, dear?" she asked her daughter.

"That's Iris, Lykenzar and Zevyn," she said, introducing them to her mother. She nodded.

Tabitha jumped on Amy. "Tabitha! You haven't changed a bit!"

"No, I haven't," Tabitha said without thinking. Amy shrieked in surprise and nearly dropped the cat.

"You can talk!" she exclaimed breathlessly.

"It's part of being a Ronen. Their bonds can talk," Zevyn explained. Carra's mother nodded, still slightly confused.

"What are you doing here?" she asked. "We'll explain later, mom." Carra said.

"Why don't you kids all come over? I'm sure there's enough space," Amy invited.

"Mom, what are *you* doing here anyway?" Carra asked.

"I just came for a vacation. I had a feeling to come here. Maybe it's because you ended up here. I guess fate has its own way of keeping us ready," her mother shrugged.

"Where are you staying?" Ron asked. "A hotel room," she cast a quick glance at the animals. "I'm not sure if they allow animals though."

"We can go back and stay outside," May suggested.

Amy nodded, and led them out of the park. "I rented a car," she explained as she unlocked a blue minivan. Everyone filed in.

She revved the engine, and the vehicle lurched forward. Ruben barely managed to fit in the seat. He was a huge hawk, and his gigantic wings, though folded, occupied a lot of space.

"What are you doing here?" Amy asked again, looking at them through the rear view mirror.

"We came to get a lotus," they explained everything. Carra's mother listened politely, without interrupting.

She let out an "Oh," in the end. She digested the information. "I'm coming with you," she said in the end.

"What!" Carra's eyes widened.

"I am. I can't let you do this on your own. Certainly not. I'm pretty sure-"

She cut herself off and swerved hard to the right as something hit the minivan hard. The car toppled on its side. Tabitha let out a hiss in alarm. Pete squawked indignantly. Ruben shook his mighty feathers, and flew out a shattered window, to deal with whatever hit them. They knew immediately that it wasn't any vehicle which hit them; it was night time, and the road had been completely empty.

Amy kicked open the passenger door and climbed out. She helped the others out. Up above, a furious battle was waging on. Ruben, a fiery ball of golden-brown, drew back and dove forward, knocking his opponent, who was also air-borne. As far as they could see in the dim light, the other bird was a pitch black smudge in the light of the moon. It screeched raucously.

Pete swooped up to join the fight. He and Ruben quickly overpowered the black bird, who was still nipping and clawing without mercy. The two birds brought down the black smudge to the ground, where Tabitha and Pal helped them to pin down the colossal bird.

Snowflake crept forward. The black bird spat at her. Its beady red eyes were brimming with hatred. It snapped its beak and lunged at the rabbit, but Tabitha raked her claws over its wings. The bird screeched in pain.

Iris knelt close to its spitting face.

"Who are you and what do you want?" she growled.

"Let go of me!" it shrieked in a high raspy voice. "Please. It's not my fault!" it sobbed. "I'm Night. They told me to attack you. I'm only following orders. If I don't, they'll kill me!"

Tabitha and Pal took a step back. Before anyone could utter a sound, the bird wrenched itself free from their grip and flew away into the oncoming darkness, laughing.

Chapter 4

They all stared, dumbfounded, as the hazy shape of the black bird vanished into the night. The moon glowed dully as they trudged the last few kilometres to the hotel.

They sat outside, on a bench. Amy sighed wearily.

"What do we do now? The car's wrecked," Josh said unhappily.

"I don't know, kids." Amy sighed again.

"Where exactly did Avaron say the lotus was?" Zevyn asked.

"He said it was in a dangerous forest, right? In an underground cave or something." Iris said.

"Where do you think that would be?" May asked.

"I know some caves around Switzerland," Josh said.

"I don't think it's there," Snowflake said quietly.

"Maybe....umm... how about in Mexico?"

"Doubt it."

"Africa?"

"Maybe."

"We could try out in some historical site, don't you think?" Iris asked.

"Yeah. Which is the most historical place, do you know, Mrs. Anderson?" Ron asked Amy.

"India!" Ruben suddenly cried out.

"What?" Iris asked her bond, confused.

Ruben stared blankly at Iris, even more dazed than the girl. "What did I just say?" he asked, blinking.

"You just said 'India'," Pal explained.

"I have never even heard of it. It just kind of flashed in my mind."

"Like someone mind-messaged you?" Josh asked, laughing.

Ruben nodded. "Seriously? I was joking!" Josh cried.

"India *does* have a good history. It was really rich in culture," Carra's mother said.

"Maybe we could try there." Pal suggested.

"Yeah, only thing is how can you get there?" Tabitha asked.

"I have a good friend in the airlines. I could ask her to give us a lift." Amy said, fishing out her mobile phone from her purse.

Lyke and Zevyn had been watching this exchange with interest.

"Where *is* India?"Lyke asked. "India is across the ocean, in the southern part of Asia," Josh replied promptly. Josh always had a good memory when it came to Geography.

Carra's mother dialled her friend. They spoke for a few moments, and then Amy cut the call.

"She said she'll be delighted to have us," Amy said with a sparkle in her eyes.

Very soon, they were at a private landing site, waiting with their luggage, which was pretty much stuff which they had just bought.

A blue and white plane gracefully landed in front of them. The door opened and a young woman popped out. She waved to them. She was tan and had a head of brown curls. Amy embraced her, and told her not to freak out if the animals talk. But she adjusted quickly, and didn't lose her nerve for a second.

"Well, get in! What are you waiting for?" the young woman called, grinning. The children and animals climbed aboard and sat comfortably. There was enough space in the back for Ruben to sit at ease, without his wings getting cramped.

The plane rolled down the runway, with Jemma, Amy's friend, called out instructions in the headset.

"Please fasten your seat belts! We are about to take off!" she called cheerfully.

Zevyn stared at the mechanism. She listened carefully as Josh and Carra explained how the plane works. Lykenzar gazed out the window, lost in his own thoughts. The animals played a game which they just invented. May, Ron and Iris joined them. Amy called Ron's father and Josh's mother to inform them that they were going to India. She filled the other two parents about everything that happened.

"Where are we going exactly, Jemma?" May asked.

"Delhi, the capital of India," the pilot called back.

May nodded and focused her attention back on the game.

* * *

"I hope they got the message," Avaron fretted.

"They would have, don't worry." His wife sat down next to him.

"So, they know where to go, don't they?" Ivy asked. She was with her family, pacing back and forth restlessly. Avaron nodded.

"Sit down, Ivy. They are fine, as you can see for yourself," Leif said. Ivy nodded absently and sat down heavily.

Minkin tore his gaze from his crystals. He and Jasper had set it up, the crystals forming a border to a pool of water. He blessed it, and a vivid scene of all of the children formed in the water.

Avaron had sent a mind message to them, and hopefully, he thought, one of them would have received it and relayed it to the others. But, something the pilot said was wrong. He couldn't find out what it was. He frowned, gazing at the crystals harder.

"What is it? What is wrong?" Raptor, Avaron's wife's bond, asked.

"That Jemma. She said something. I cannot put my finger on it." He bit his lip. After a moment of intense thinking, he sighed.

"You will get to know, don't worry," Victoria said. "And when you do, it will not be too late for you to change their course."

Chapter 5

"The flight's landed! You have my permission to remove your seatbelts. Please get up and move out in single file, arms stiff. Now, march!" Jemma joked, jumping out of her seat. She gave a huge grin to Pete as he flew out.

"I prefer to use my own wings to this artificial set," Ruben grumbled as he clambered to the door.

"Don't worry, you'll get used to it." Jemma flashed him an encouraging smile, and walked to the end. She ushered the rest of the animals outside. She had grown very fond of all the animals, and she kept asking them to visit her again.

"We'll try, don't worry," Tabitha purred. Pal licked her arm. "Thanks for the ride, Jem. You're an amazing pilot!"

"Aww, thanks, Pal."

"I'll miss you," Snowflake said. "I'll miss you too. I hope to see you again soon."

They all said their farewells and stood back. Jemma entered her plane and took off.

They walked out of the clearing, and were immediately pushed into a bustling crowd. Pete and Ruben immediately took refuge in the sky. May and Zevyn picked up Tabitha and Snowflake before they were trampled. Nobody took any heed of the group of foreigners. They walked on, the sounds of hundreds of shopkeepers shouting for attention getting to them.

They managed to make it to a quiet corner, where the children collapsed on the two benches there. Pete and Ruben joined them.

"India's a big country. I wonder where we should even start searching for the lotus," Josh sighed. His friends nodded in agreement. Amy was busy making a phone call.

"Here's a good place as any," May said.

"I doubt it would be in such a commercial place," Lyke said.

Zevyn shook her head. "The lotus was kept like a millennium before this town or city or whatever even developed."

"I do not think it was that long ago. Lyke does have a point," Iris said. Lyke gave his sister an I-told-you-so look.

"Karnataka!" Ron burst out.

"What-a-kata?" Carra asked, confused. She put a hand on her cousin's forehead. "Ron, are you ill or something?"

"No. Karnataka. Karnataka," he repeated. Carra looked at Josh. He shrugged and turned his attention back to Ron, who was still mumbling 'Karnataka' over and over.

"What did you say, Ron?" Amy had hung up, and was looking at her nephew.

"Karnataka," he said again, looking at his aunt. Her eyes flew wide open.

"Karnataka's a state of India!" she said, smiling broadly.

Pal turned to look at his bond. "Ron, you're a genius!"

"Well done, Ron," Zevyn said. Iris grinned at him.

"What did I just say?" Ron asked, suddenly wondering why he was getting so much attention.

"It must be Avaron. He must be sending us mind messages! That is why India flashed to me!" Ruben suddenly said, his eyes betraying his excitement.

Iris nodded in agreement.

"Well then. To Karnataka!" Amy said jovially, and the band set off to find the airport.

* * *

"Well?" the Shadow snarled in Avaron's face. The leader didn't flinch. Instead, he spat at the Death Lord.

"You don't deserve to even exist on any planet. You should end your miserable, vile existence," the Ronen leader hissed.

"I should now, should I?" the Shadow of Death purred silkily, winding his mist-like body around Avaron. "And why don't you help me?" he continued, curling his thorn-like claws under Avaron's chin.

"Do you think me to be so helpless, so pitiful, so weak, to not see past your devious but meagre attempts to stall me? Do you think that I would fall for that same old trick your tribe tried to use? What do you think of me, the Great Shadow, the Powerful Death Lord, the all mighty Shadow of Death?" He brought his claws down and scratched the stone on the floor, leaving a long trail of claw marks.

"I think you are a plain old idiot," Avaron muttered under his breath, but not loud enough for the gloating Lord to hear.

It had been two and a half days since the children left. Half a day after Minkin returned to the camp, the Death Lord had barged into the camp, striding straight to where the leader stood. The Shadow's hideous army had wreaked havoc across the Ronen territory. The Shadow had tried every day to extract information from every single Ronen.

The winged boy scuttled up to the impatient Lord.

"What do you want now, you impeccable nuisance?" the Shadow growled. The boy stretched up to reach the Lord's face and muttered something. The Lord's face widened in a grin of pleasure, but immediately vanished.

"Of course. I had thought of that too, and I was just going to implement it," he said triumphantly. Avaron rolled his eyes. The pompous Lord refused to let anything pass him by!

The Shadow of Death turned to face Avaron. Lord faced leader, both spitting vengeance on each other.

The shadow leaned forward, until his mist-like face was inches from Avaron's.

"This is not over. I will defeat you. And when I do, I *will* kill you!"

Chapter 6

"*That* was a horrible flight!" Lyke groaned.

"Totally agree," Josh said. They had arrived in the city of Bangalore, and were in a taxi cab to civilization.

They arrived soon, and the greedy taxi driver demanded his money. Amy quickly gave him the taxi fare and climbed off. The taxi sped away into the distance, leaving a gust of wind and dust swirling around them.

Ron coughed. "What a (cough) meano!" he exclaimed, waving the dust away from him with his hand.

"Come on, we're wasting time!" May urged, pulling their luggage and Snowflake's cage behind her. The flight and police authorities had insisted on keeping the rabbit, Pete, Ruben and Tabitha in a cage and Pal on a leash at all times. But as soon as they arrived, Iris let Ruben free. He immediately took to his blue haven.

"Where do we go now?" Ron asked.

"Let's go get a hotel first. Then we'll see about the lotus," Amy insisted.

"Where's a hotel?" Ron demanded.

"We can ask that driver of that weird thing, maybe," Carra suggested, looking pointedly at a man standing beside an auto rickshaw.

"Hmm."

The group crossed the road and stood in front of the driver. He looked up from the newspaper he was reading.

"Can you please tell us the way to the nearest hotel where we can stay?" Amy asked politely.

The auto driver said something incomprehensible to the group.

"Excuse me?"

Suddenly, Zevyn said something to the auto driver in another language and he replied. Everybody stared at her except Lykenzar, who puffed out his chest with pride.

"She has the gift of tongues," he said importantly.

"Why didn't you use it before?" May asked curiously.

"Well, I don't know it all the time. When I need it, it just flashes and I know the language by-heart."

"What did he say?" Iris asked.

"We have to go a bit down this road, take the right next to a medical shop, and on the left side, one house before the road ends, is the hotel," she said.

They followed her instructions and came to a hotel. Carra's mother eyed it critically. Then she shrugged and led the way in.

Zevyn quickly spoke with the manager, and handed over a room key to Amy. But before they could go, the manager said something else. Zevyn clarified it, and turned to her friends.

"Sorry, guys," she held her hands up apologetically. "No animals allowed here."

Carra groaned.

"Then where do we keep them?" Iris demanded.

The manager walked up to them. Speaking in broken English, he said that they could leave the animals in the pet shop opposite the hotel.

Amy thanked him, and hustled the group out of the hotel. The children followed grudgingly; none of them were happy at the thought of being separated from their bonds.

They made their farewells short, and returned to the hotel quickly.

The next morning, the group checked out, and quickly collected the animals. They purchased a map from a local store and stood on the side of the narrow street to study it.

"Hmm. We're... here, I think," Carra's mother mused.

"Maybe we should check out a library to see the most historical places here," Lyke suggested. Pal grunted softly in agreement. As if his barks had summoned them, two stray dogs shot out of their places from under a car and stood menacingly in front of Pal, snarling. Pal stared back, confused.

"We'd better go," Zevyn said uncertainly. Amy nodded, and the group set off swiftly, Ron glancing back now and then to see if the dogs were still pursuing his bond. Thankfully, they left them when they rounded the corner of the street. Lyke and Zevyn glanced at each other in puzzlement.

"Let's keep moving," Iris said with a worried glance behind her back.

Carra's mother nodded, and led the group away. They paused briefly to check the map again, and made their way to the nearest library.

They left Lykenzar, Ron and Iris outside with the animals. Once inside, they asked the librarian for historical books. She showed them and walked back to her desk, smiling at them.

The group rooted out every possible book which had a possibility of giving them their answer. After a strenuous hour of searching, May finally triumphantly shouted out, "I've got it!"

The others immediately bunched around her. "See?" she said pointing out the page. "It's right there. Hampi," she said. The others nodded. Zevyn took the book from May and read it out loud.

Amy nodded when she finished. "You're right. We should go there as soon as possible."

Suddenly, her phone rang. She picked it up, and talked quickly. When she cut the call, she looked very excited.

"What is it?" Carra asked her mother.

"Ron's dad just called. He's here it seems. He left Jessica in Josh's house. He has a very close friend in Bangalore, and we can stay there for the night, and tomorrow, we can all leave for Hampi."

They placed all the books back as soon as they could, and thanking the librarian, they shuffled out. They told the others the news.

"Cool!" Ron said, apparently amazed at how fast news travelled. Lykenzar nodded approvingly, while Iris resorted to talking excitedly to Ruben.

Ron's dad picked them up from a hotel. As they drove, they filled him in on other details.

The journey to the neighbourhood of Ron's dad's friend was one hour. The car was an eight-seater; but still there wasn't enough space for all of them. Ruben and Pete flew overhead, while the others were still congested. Ron's father drove, Carra's mother sat in the passenger seat with Tabitha. Behind them, the children were stuffed with the luggage.

They stopped many times to readjust themselves with the luggage, and it took them a little over three hours to reach their destination.

Finally, the car pulled over in front of a big house. An aging man, around 50 years old at guess, opened the front door and rushed out to meet them.

"Ajay!" Ron's dad called, waving as he pulled out a small suitcase.

"Max!" he shouted back, his Indian accent sounding slightly strange to the friends.

Max quickly introduced all of them to each other.

"Ajay was my colleague before he retired. He is a close friend of mine," he explained. Turning to his friend, he asked, "Are you sure you don't mind us staying?"

"No, no, not at all," he chuckled. "You are all welcome. The animals too, though Kamala will probably want to cover the furniture before they come in." Grinning broadly, he led them inside.

Chapter 7

The Shadow Lord drifted past where Avaron was tied up. The Ronen leader recoiled at the stench which followed the black figure.

Avaron turned to see his eldest daughter, who was being forced to toil at building weapons with the other Ronens. Sharp squeals occasionally accompanied the clanging of metal against metal as they worked hard under the cruel eye of the Shadow's captains.

Leif, Avaron's son, paused for a minute to wipe his brow, but was rewarded with a lash to his back from a whip. He glared at his tormentor, but continued to work nevertheless.

The Shadow suddenly whipped around and fixed his cold gaze on Avaron.

"You are going to regret this," he hissed, his ever-changing form wrapped around himself, and a clawed hand slashed out from the mist which formed the Shadow's body. The hand came inches to Avaron's face, but it retreated.

The Death Lord ranted off about another long twisted story about how the future was going to be glorious, for him, of course, not for Avaron. But the Ronen leader wasn't listening to him, he switched his mind to the children he'd sent back to Earth.

He remembered how he had sent them mind messages to tell them where they would find the treasure. But as his train of thought grew longer, he became wearier. His eyelids drooped, and he drifted off to sleep.

He woke up with a start. The Shadow flashed past him in a blur of black. Avaron tried to retreat, but found himself backed against a solid wall. He turned around, but saw the forest instead. Then he realized; the wall was there, but not there. *Quantum physics*, he thought vaguely.

Another blur and a slap to the face brought him back to the problem at hand- Shadow of Death. He struck out with his foot, hoping to trip the Shadow, but he just floated past. When Avaron brought his foot back, he was shocked to see that it was decayed. His eyes widened, and his heart thumped so loud, he thought the Death Lord could hear it.

He bolted up straight out of his sleep, his face awash with perspiration. He checked his foot immediately; it was fine, no sign of decay or rot. *It was a dream*, he thought. Realization hit him as sharp as an arrow. *If we try to fight back against him, we will also rot away. We should escape. But how?*

Chapter 8

"Try this. It is my wife's specialty," Ajay invited. It was dinner time, and they were eyeing the table hungrily. Ajay's servant had taken the animals outside for their dinner. He had bought food for all of them.

The animals had not talked since they entered the house, not wanting to give the old couple a fright.

After they had arrived at the house, Iris had received a vision; the same one as her father had dreamt, though this was unknown to her. She was backed against an invisible wall, and a blur threatened her life. She couldn't identify it, but she had a doubt that it was the Shadow. She had tried to fight him, but ended up having a decayed hand when she tried to fight off the blur.

Iris had freaked out then, and it took her a long time to recover. She was sure that her family was in trouble, and she almost stormed out of the house to search for the lotus on her own. It took all of them to restrain her. She had calmed down eventually, but the vision still haunted her.

At the moment, she was very grave at the dinner table, refusing to speak to anyone but Ruben. The Indian couple didn't understand her resolution, but they didn't press her. Instead, the kind hearted duo tried to distract her by giving delicious dishes for her to try. Slowly, she shook off her misery and enjoyed dinner.

Ajay and his wife gave them three guest rooms. Kamala seemed a little hesitant to let the animals sleep inside, but Ajay persuaded her until she agreed. They ate their dessert- an ice cream which their servant had hurriedly purchased- and were soon snoring in their rooms.

They had woken up early the next morning to find that Kamala had prepared a feast for them to eat then, and also for the journey to Hampi. Ajay even offered them to take his car, seeing that they barely had enough space for everyone.

They agreed, and the two adults sat behind the wheel and they were off.

❋ ❋ ❋

Ruben suddenly started screeching and clawed at the window next to him. It was mid-day, and they were on a lonely highway.

The others in the same car looked at Ruben in shock. The usually calm hawk was suddenly acting like his life depended on getting out of the car. Iris reached out and slid open the window and her bond flew out in a rush of feathers.

They all peered out the window. Ruben flew up and collided with an incoming bullet speed of black.

“What’s going on?” Carra’s mother, who was driving, halted the car. Behind them, Max’s car also squealed to a stop.

Iris opened the car door and jumped out. The others crowded around her. They squinted upwards, trying to see what was going on against the sun’s bright rays.

Shrill shrieks echoed around as the battle waged on. With a last screech, the black smudge accepted defeat and half flew, half fell to the earth. Ruben followed, clawing the falling bird one last time. Just before it landed, Ruben snatched it in his strong grip and laid it almost gently on the ground. The others all rushed to see.

As they got a better look at what Ruben had attacked, Zevyn gasped. “It’s the same bird which pushed the minivan in Scotland!”

Ruben nodded.

"You just saved our lives!" Tabitha exclaimed.

Iris hugged her bond. "It was probably going to knock us off again."

May leaned closer to the bird's face. Slowly, in agony, it opened its eyes.

"Why did you try to attack us *again*? You promised!" Carra hissed.

"Why didn't you just give up?" Snowflake snarled.

The bird just groaned and let its head fall.

Lyke gasped. "Is it dead?"

"No," Ruben growled. "She is a crafty one. She is just trying to trick us. Again."

"She?"

"The Death Lord sent her. She said he wanted us dead, and that she was the best assassin," he explained.

"Yeah right. Ruben would have made a better assassin, if he ever had the heart to even take up such an offer," Josh snorted.

"Should we treat her?" Ron asked cautiously. Pal looked at him exasperatedly.

"Better kill her. But, we aren't so cruel. Why don't we just give her to a zoo? After all, where has one seen such a bird?"

The others looked at the limp bird. It was true. She was big, very big, with red eyes. The tips of her tail and wings were white, while her claws were an unexpected pale brown. Her neck had rings of white, and her beak was spotted.

"That's a good idea. She'd be better off in captivity," Max agreed. The bird squawked in surprise.

Ruben looked at the others in contempt. The bird realized her mistake and pretended to act dead again.

"So much for playing dead." Josh sneered. He resisted the urge to kick her, and instead hefted her over his shoulder by a wing. She let out a whimper of pain. Lyke held another wing, while Ron provided support for her scarred claws. Together, the three boys carried the huge bird to one of the cars, where Max immediately tied her up with bits of rope he found.

"Now all we need is a zoo," he announced.

After about half an hour, they were face to face with a nearby zoo's veterinarian, who had immediately asked his assistant to take custody of the bird. He had marvelled at the intricate patterns in the rings of white on its neck, but decided to examine it later, once she was treated.

Amy and Max spoke to the vet; they had left the children and the animals in the cars.

They cast one last glance at the bird. She had looked back at them pitifully, but they glared at her coldly. She dropped her head, losing all hope.

They were on the road once more. A few kilometres away from the zoo, they stopped to clean a bloody Ruben up. He stood still as they dabbed paper dripping with water around his neck. He was pretty badly wounded, but he had fared much better than his adversary.

Finally, when they had cleaned him up, they proceeded with their journey. Ruben was still wet, and Tabitha refused to sit next to him no matter what. Pal ended up next to Ruben, and the dog revelled in the hawk's dampness, enjoying the moisture seeping into his fur.

They stopped for lunch in a highway hotel. The animals were left staring wistfully at their bonds as the children and the adults went inside the restaurant. After they finished their lunch, they bought a parcel meal for their bonds and waited as the animals wolfed down their lunch.

They drove again, halting for a break a couple of hours after lunch to stretch their legs/paws/wings.

They set out again. The children stared at the lonely highway, and a pang of homesickness hit them. Ruben and Pete flew out, relishing the feeling of wind in their feathers. Pal peeped out of the window, panting in the face of the breeze. Tabitha and snowflake curled up together, while the children played games in their separate cars.

It grew darker, and the children got bored of their games. They decided to try to communicate through the cars. But it started raining, and they abandoned that hope. Ruben and Pete rushed back to the cars. The light rain turned into a wild storm, and they were forced to pull over. They parked side by side, and the children told horror tales.

Thunder roared ahead, and only the momentary lightning showed the surroundings. The two adults tried to locate where exactly they were, but there was no signal, and the battery of their torches had died out.

They distributed shawls and jackets to keep warm against the growing chill.

The animals huddled against the children to keep them warm, but it didn't block out all the cold. The children shivered as they tried to fall asleep.

The thudding of rain on the car roof top kept Pal awake. So he was the only one to realize that there was mist spreading around the cars, and strange lights flickering amidst the fog.

Chapter 9

"Wake up!"

"What?" Ivy asked groggily. She was lying on the cold floor next to Avaron's feet. Leif lay beside his sister, and he too stirred. He saw the urgency in his father's eyes, and quickly shoved Ivy into full consciousness. She sat up in a heartbeat, but Leif pulled her back down.

"Do you *want* every guard here to know that we are going to escape?" he hissed fiercely. She quickly apologized softly, and looked around over her brother's shoulder. Once she saw that it was quiet, she turned her attention to her father, who was still looking annoyed that she had woken up only after he called her about a dozen times. She shrugged apologetically to her father; a movement she hoped hadn't alerted the nearby guard.

"Come on," Leif whispered. He slowly slid across the floor, finding it a little difficult under the bulk of the stuffing he had worn to look like his father.

It had been two days since Avaron had received his dream. He had figured out a plan then- Leif was to dress up as him, while he would escape to get help. Leif would not be missed; he had not done anything to stand out. Avaron had managed to untie his hands; it was much easier to remove the knots that bound his legs together.

Now that the plan was finally in action, Avaron felt a little nervous. Leif finally reached his father. He quickly took up the leader's place, and as Ivy helped her father tie her brother to the tree, she could not help but marvel at how similar Leif and Avaron looked. At first, it was doubted that the plan could work-Avaron was hefty and had broad shoulders, while Leif was thin and lean like his mother. But with all the extra padding, the two were as similar as the mud on the ground.

Avaron looked up briefly, glad to see that the sentry on duty hadn't noticed anything strange, and kept staring into the distance, while his companion snored at his post. The Ronen leader grunted with amusement, and bade a hasty farewell to his son and daughter. Then he made his way out, breaking into a run once among the thicker and denser trees.

As dawn broke out, he was sure that he had made it away safely. *But do not be too sure*, he reminded himself. The Death Lord was a tricky one. He had spies throughout Imagneus.

He jogged on, pushing past undergrowths and moving on trails he had never explored before. But as he neared a small clearing, he heard a rustling sound. He spun around, dreading that it was one of the Shadow's minions, come to take him back. Instead, two faces, so familiar he cried out in surprise, emerged from behind a tree.

"Chester! Romial! What are you doing here?"

Chester bounded forward.

"What do you expect? That your bond should sit and do nothing while you endanger your life on a quest that has more options of failing than succeeding? Absolutely not!"

Romial nodded in agreement.

Avaron sighed, and felt a smile warming his face. "Of course you can join me. I could not ask for better companions than the two of you."

"Well then. Shall we move on? Where are we going first?" Romial asked.

"I thought of gathering the tribes and clans of every place to help us in this battle. After all, we are united against this threat."

His travelling companions nodded. "There is sense in that," Romial agreed. "Let us proceed then, and rid this planet of that filthy creature once and for all!"

"We reached!" Chester cried out, waving his tail excitedly. Romial and Avaron nodded wearily. They were going to meet the queen of Hikints. They shuffled towards the city lying in front of them. A sentry at the gates widened his eyes in surprise at the sight of the Ronen leader and deputy together. He quickly ushered them in, calling for another soldier to escort them. They nodded thankfully at the sentry and followed the soldier to meet the queen of the Hikints.

As they walked down the little streets of the Hikint town, Avaron remembered how the Hikints had taken ideas from the humans to build their cities. A few passer bys looked at them in surprise, but no comments were passed.

They finally arrived at the beautiful carved door of the queen's castle. The soldier politely knocked, and the doors swung open, revealing a magnificent hall, decorated with exotic plants. Avaron and his companions marvelled at the complexity of the structure.

The trio, led by another soldier, entered the palace, and made their way to the Hearing Hall; the hall where the queen settled disputes and responded to complaints.

As they set foot inside the hall, the queen rose from her seat, astonished.

"Avaron! What a surprise!" she smiled. Avaron nodded respectfully. The common folk rose from their seats in respect.

"Please, have a seat," the queen invited. Avaron led his companions to the front and whispered, "We need to talk to you; it is very important." The queen nodded immediately, and quickly told her minister to postpone the meeting. She rose elegantly from her seat and led the way to a chamber.

Once seated, Avaron launched into a detailed story of everything that had happened. Romial and Chester took over the story when he paused. The queen listened intently, not interrupting till their tale was finished. She was silent for some time, thinking over what they had just told her.

"We will gladly help," she said at last. "This danger threatens not only your clan, but every other tribe in this planet. I will send one of my people with you, so that you have more chances of getting help."

Avaron almost rolled his eyes. *She just wants to show that she is helping us so much. She obviously will want a return favour after this.*

But instead, he said, "Thank you so much for your help. I will not forget this."

Chester flicked his ear, looking slightly irritated that Avaron seemed to be actually genuine, when it was clear that all that the queen wanted was a chance to show herself great. But Avaron caught his bond's eye, and he understood that the leader thought the same.

The trio bid their farewell and exited the gate, with a young soldier Hikint behind them.

Avaron and Romial took the lead, with the Hikint behind them, and Chester bringing up the rear. Romial questioned the Hikint, and after the third attempt, managed to find out the shy Hikint's name, but forgot it immediately, so long was his name. After asking again, the Hikint told them to call him Sabre. Avaron was surprised, finding the name Sabre a bit too savage for the shy Hikint, but didn't comment.

As dusk fell, they decided to stop for a rest, and make camp. Sabre offered to keep watch while the others slept, and they agreed. They quickly ate, and the three Ronens slept, leaving Sabre to stand guard.

They woke at dawn, surprised to see Sabre standing over a weird creature, which was bound up. Avaron felt his doubts disappear. *Sabre is not only good, he is so silent! None of us woke up, and he didn't wake us up either. He is smart,* Avaron thought.

They disposed of the creature and continued their journey.

They managed to rally help from half a dozen other tribes, and set their attack on the next Night of Faztex.

Chapter 10

"What in the world *is* that?" the children had woken with Pal's repeated barking, and were astonished to see the mist clouding around them. Strange lights-blue, green and red-were glowing mysteriously in the midst of the fog. Ron's father had offered to check it out, but none of the others agreed.

"What do we do?" Snowflake asked.

Ron shrugged, shivering. Ruben also offered to check out the lights.

"What if they are not dangerous? I will not take long, I promise. Besides, what is the harm in just looking around quickly? We can go together." He argued, motioning to Max. The adult had agreed, and grudgingly, Iris allowed her bond to venture outside.

Ruben crept outside, immediately vanishing behind the haze. He flew close to one of the lights, which was flickering eerily. Ron's father was right next to the hawk, bending down to inspect it.

The light blinked at him, and disappeared, in its place, a little piece of folded up paper. The two looked at each other, and made their way back to the two cars. Once inside, they opened the paper, and found spidery writing all over the page.

Dear Lotus seekers,

I am the guardian of the Lotus. Kindly give up all attempts to gain the Lotus from my grasp, for it will be fruitless. But, however, if you do persist, there may be a certain way to achieve your mission, though it will be dangerous, and I highly recommend you give up now. If you fail that mission, I assure you your journey will end in Heaven (or Hell). But if you finish it, then maybe I can compromise something. But beware; this will be by far the toughest mission you would have ever faced. The mission

"There are some stains after that. I can't make out anything else." Max said sadly.

The others looked downcast, none of them making a sound. Pal was the first to break the silence.

"How did that thing, whatever it is, actually find out who we are, and what we are looking for?" he asked, looking frightened and bewildered. The others shrugged.

"What if it's spying on us?" Pete asked.

"How can it? We've never seen it." Josh said.

Tabitha nodded. "The only one we've actually seen is the crow, whatever thing. And she's been taken care of."

"Maybe it is hiding in the fog?" Iris suggested.

"But how can it mindread us?" Zevyn argued.

"You have the gift of tongues, don't you?" Carra asked her suddenly.

"Yes, but I can't sense stuff," Zevyn retorted.

"What about you Lyke? Do you have any special powers or anything?" Ron asked hopefully. He shook his head. "Only Zevyn," he confirmed.

It seemed as if everyone who was present there drooped, all hopes of figuring out what the strange warning meant was burnt.

"Hey!" May said, suddenly shooting straight up. "Hi," Pal said automatically, but then regretted it as everyone glared at him.

"Well, what is it?" Amy prompted.

"You got that paper when you touched the light, didn't you?" Max and Ron nodded.

"Maybe, if you get more papers, we can find out what this means!" she said, jiggling around in excitement. The others looked at each other happily.

"Great thinking, May!" Carra's mother patted her.

"Awesome idea. We'll go now," Max announced, looking over at Ruben, who was ruffling up his feathers. The hawk nodded, and the two exited the car in a flash.

They came back soon, each bearing at least two papers each. All had the same spidery handwriting, but a different message.

Dear Lotus Seekers,

It is better if you end this goose chase now. If you don't, here's a riddle for you to solve. Decode it, and I will grant you permission to move on.

AN ARROW WILL GUIDE YOU TO A SHRINE

THE SHRINE OF STONE HAS A FERRY FINE

SET SAIL ON IT SLOWLY AND YOU WILL FIND

MAYBE, IT'S NOT JUST A TRICK OF THE MIND.

Have fun with the riddle. But always keep in mind that this hunt is much more dangerous than you think.

The Guardian.

"The rhyme makes no sense!" May protested when they finished reading the first riddle.

Max shrugged. "There's nothing to do other than follow it."

"Read the second one," Snowflake suggested. They turned to the next scroll. The second one didn't waste ink on greetings. It jumped straight to the point.

So, you're puzzled by my little rhyme. Read this one, and maybe things will get a little clearer.

STARRY SKIES GRIEVE, LAMENT AND CRY

WHILE YOU ENTER THE LAGOON; GO ON, DON'T BE SHY

DOWN THE STEPS- 273 YOU GO AND STAND BY

REACH A CRANNY, SAY, AND SHOUT HI!

"What? This is more confusing than the last!" Tabitha cried.

"We'd better read all. Then maybe we can get a hang of things." Amy said, slightly worried.

Well, if you're still confused, why not give this rhyme a go?

SHOUT IF YOU MUST, TO GET YOUR BEARINGS

BUT SHOUT LOUD, I'M HARD OF HEARING

LOOK TO THE SKY, BUT DON'T TRY STARING,

AN ARROW WILL APPEAR TO SEE HOW YOU'RE FARING!

"Is that the arrow mentioned in the first riddle?" Iris asked. Zevyn nodded. "Could be."

Ruben handed the last scroll to Ron's dad.

Try and figure this out. I think you are getting somewhere. But this is a warning, the rhymes as you read were not in order. Please try keep up.

IT'S GETTING WET, AND COLD AND DARK

EVERYTHING SAID SEEMS LIKE AN ECHOING BARK

DON'T BE TERRIFIED, IT'S NOT A SHARK,

BUT BE AFRAID, IT'S NOT AS GENTLE AS A LARK.

"This is getting really confusing," Pete muttered, resting on Pal. "Maybe, the third one we read is the first," Pal ventured. Pete shot up straight. "You're right!" he squawked. "And the first one we read is the second, and then we have to set sail, right? So we'll end up in water-"

"And then go into a lagoon and everything becomes cold and wet, and there's something dangerous over there, but not as dangerous as a shark!" Tabitha continued excitedly.

"We have to try that," Lyke said. The others murmured their agreement.

"But where exactly is that water? And a stone with a ferry? What does that mean?"

"I guess we're supposed to find a huge stone with a ferry inside it."

"We'd better just get there; we'll see what we can do later."

Chapter 11

"I am so bored," Ron grumbled.

"But we were just playing!" Iris protested.

The group were still on the journey to Hampi. It was the day after they had found the scrolls. Earlier that morning, they had taken the advice of the rhyme and shouted loudly to the Guardian, then looked at the sky for any sign of the arrow. Finally, after almost half an hour of searching the sky for the arrow, they realized that it wasn't even an arrow, it was the name of the place they had to get to; it was written 'Hampi' clearly, formed by the clouds.

"I'm hungry," Pal whined. "You always are," Snowflake sniffed.

"But I am too!" Ron joined in. Max shot his son a glare before handing over a rucksack of food to the boy. Ron's eyes gleamed as he scouted through the contents of the bag.

They feasted on the sandwiches they had brought. Finally, after another couple of hours of driving, they reached the city of Hampi.

"Now for a hotel," Amy announced. They drove through the old village, stopping in front of a good-looking hotel. The adults entered, leaving the children and the animals in the cars. Inside, they asked the clerk about the major attractions of Hampi. He handed them a booklet, explaining rapidly.

Thanking him, they exited the hotel with the booklet and climbed into their cars. Once they reached a spot where nobody would see them, they all gathered together.

"The riddle is about a shrine. It's given in this that the stone chariot here," Carra's mother pointed to its picture on the booklet, "was built as a shrine for a god. It's made of stone, as given, and is the only one which is relatively close to a ferry, because it's a chariot."

"That's awesome!" Josh cried out, his eyes shining.

"We're nearly there!" Lyke agreed, slapping his sister a hi-five.

"Let's get this show on the road," Tabitha mewed, lifting her paws impatiently. They set off, driving to the stone chariot.

When they reached, they jumped out of the cars, vying with each other to be the first to land. Ruben shook his feathers and shot into the sky like a rocket, Pete following more slowly. Pal bounded out excitedly, with Ron chasing him to put on a leash. Iris scooped up Snowflake, before joining the others.

They looked around in awe. The buildings were intricately carved; there were horses, elephants, soldiers, kings, slaves, dancers and many more decorating the walls of the Vittala temple next to the stone chariot. They gazed at the architecture in admiration, forgetting about the rhymes for a moment. They came out of their trance when a dog nearby started howling.

Pal whipped his head around. A young boy was throwing stones at a black and tan dog. Pal growled, but Ron held him back. Before the group could scold the boy, the dog gave a low menacing bark before turning away. A local guide marched up to the boy and dragged him away by the ear. The boy whimpered in pain, but knew better than to scream in public.

"Serves him right." Pal muttered. Lyke nodded, and they made their way to the stone chariot.

"You know, I think it's better if we return at midnight. What can we do with everybody here?" Zevyn murmured. Max agreed, and led the group away. They waited in the cars until the moon was up, shining brightly, and stealthily re-entered the temple grounds.

The moon was almost full, casting a bright glow on the chariot. They tip-toed around to the back of the chariot and started inspecting it.

"What are we even supposed to be looking for?" May asked.

"A ferry? Or something like that, I guess," Zevyn shrugged. Carra's mother nodded.

"But there is no ferry or a boat on this," Ruben said, puzzled.

"What if it's on the inside?" Ron asked.

"Inside?"

"You know, up that ladder thingy out front, inside this temple thing."

"Worth a try, I suppose."

Pete flew inside, and searched the interior. The children climbed in, and started searching beside the parrot. Ron tried to go to the back of the shrine, but tripped over Josh who was trying to go out. Ron fell down, and grabbed a piece of rock which was poking out, to save himself from falling inside a hole which somehow just appeared. He screamed. Lyke grabbed his hand and pulled him away.

"Thank you!" he breathed, and screamed again.

"I've got to hand it to you, bro, you may be stupid, but you are clever!" Josh said, patting Ron's back.

"But that doesn't make sense!" Carra argued.

"I don't care." Josh shrugged. They jumped out, and told those waiting outside of the events. Max hugged his son.

"I think we are supposed to go inside that hole. Maybe the ferry is waiting over there." Iris murmured.

They climbed into the chariot.

"One of us should go there first and check it out," Pete said.

"I will go," Ruben volunteered. Before his bond could protest, he added, "If there is danger, I can just fly out. It would be harder for you."

Reluctantly Iris agreed, and Ruben swooped down silently, clutching a flashlight in his talons.

From above, they could see only the dancing pattern of the flashlight beam. Soon, Ruben appeared at the edge of the opening.

"It is safe," he reported.

"How far is it?" Zevyn asked.

"There's a ladder about a metre from the edge. At the bottom, there is a very small strip of land. Do not get down there. When you are on the last rung of the ladder, jump to the left, backwards. It is solid ground there," he cautioned.

Max went first. Right above, Lyke climbed down, followed by his sister, who was guiding Tabitha down. Ruben led them, offering advice. When Max reached the last rung, the hawk helped him, guiding him with his wing tips. Tabitha, on Zevyn's back, nimbly jumped down.

Snowflake was right behind the cat, carried by May. Josh and Ron together managed to just keep Pal from falling. The golden retriever got stuck in the middle though, and Ruben, with Lyke's help, managed to carry the dog to safety. Ron and Josh descended quickly after that. Carra and her mother were last, with Pete bringing the rear. Above them, the hole closed as suddenly as it had opened.

Chapter 12

"Weapons ready?"

The gruff voice of the general Streo brought Avaron back to reality. He looked around, shaking away the worries of his Ronens. The Streo troops were engaged in a mock combat, in training for the war against the Shadow.

"March! Single line! Battle position, steady now. Aim, fire!" the steady drone of the general's commands rang out in the air.

At the general's order, a shower of arrows rained on the battlefield, which was full of dummy enemies.

A couple of soldiers scuttled along the battleground, picking up the arrows. They quickly retreated as another bunch of arrows flew across the sky and embedded themselves in the tough soil.

On the far side, a group of Streos were duelling with swords. The lash of metal echoed around the clearing. On yet another corner, some Streos were racing around a very intense obstacle course.

Avaron walked around to join the duelling Streos. He was content now that he could finally prepare himself for the battle. He picked up a sword and entered the ring. No sooner had he stood inside than two Streos rushed at him, their swords raised. But Avaron held his ground, batting one away easily and blocking the blow of the second in one swipe. The general had ordered this kind of training, so that if enemies rushed them off guard, they still had a chance of winning.

Another Streo joined forces with Avaron, and together, matching blow for blow, they forced the attacking Streos back. The attackers accepted defeat, and the four wiped their brows as they searched for other opponents.

A sharp ringing stopped all matches. Everyone dropped their weapons in a heap and filed into a tent from which a delicious aroma wafted out.

They stood in a line, as they waited for their turn at the food table. Romial and Chester joined Avaron, and the three stood at the back.

They joined the table of the Streos who had just finished the obstacle race. They were still panting after the tiring exercise, but that didn't stop them from chattering away.

"When do you think we are going to be ready?" Chester whispered to his bond.

"You know that we are going to fight back on the Night of Faztex, but we have a better chance if the children get back before that day."

Chester nodded, his mind immediately picturing the children.

"Are you sure that they can do it?" Chester asked after a moment's hesitation.

"Never doubt them, Chester. Do not forget, they had accomplished the mission against Grinlaut in the best manner. And anyhow they do have Carra's mother and Ron's father with them," Avaron reassured his bond. Chester dipped his head in agreement.

A female soldier walked up to Avaron. Bending her head in greeting, she introduced herself as one of the highest ranking captains. Avaron nodded, though inwardly, he was slightly confused at the Streo's elaborate army plan. There were soldiers, chiefs, commanders, generals, captains, and finally, the leader, all in hierarchy, though he did not know the order.

"I just wanted to know the complete battle plan," The female captain continued. Seeing the suspicious glint in Romial's eyes, she added hastily, "So that my troops can be ready for anything." Pausing, she stood up straight. "I need to prepare my troops for the most dangerous enemy. That is what I have got my captaincy for. I'm not the best for nothing. And I need to know exactly what to do in the battle field." She looked at Avaron with a challenge in her eyes.

Avaron just blinked in agreement. The female warrior narrowed her eyes.

"I am very sorry to disappoint you, but we have no plan," he said simply.

"And maybe you should cut down on your speeches. It saves us from boredom," Chester whispered to Romial. Romial chuckled softly but stopped when the glare that the captain was giving to Avaron turned on him.

"We are yet to discuss that with your leader. We cannot tell you silly fairytales, now, can we?" Romial asked slyly.

With a final glare, the female warrior stomped off.

"Well, we managed to damage her pride. What does she think of herself?" Romial growled. Chester sniffed in agreement.

"Do not think bad about her. She was just doing her duty," Avaron chided.

"Does that mean she can get so pompous?"

"She is probably used to getting respect from everyone. She might find it tough to give respect as well."

"It does not hurt to change."

"You are right, but maybe we should give her some space. I saw her leading the troops the other day. She fights well."

"That is probably the only reason they gave her the post of 'one of the highest ranking captains,'" Romial mimicked.

Both Chester and Avaron chuckled at his excellent imitation of the haughty warrior.

"But actually, she does have a point. We had better go to the leader right after lunch and discuss the plan." Avaron said after a moment.

Romial shrugged nonchalantly. Chester shook out his mane. They finished their food, and made their way to the leader's residence.

They knocked, and the door opened almost immediately. The leader stood there, wearing a grim expression. Romial looked surprised that even the leader was a battle-scarred female. He had never seen the leader before, as he had been training when Avaron and Chester first met her.

She invited them inside, and Avaron introduced Romial to the leader. After that he got straight to the point. The leader thought over their words.

"So it all depends on the children?" she asked. Avaron nodded, suddenly realizing how much the children carried on their shoulders.

Miva remained quiet for some time. Suddenly, her eyes lighted up. She walked over to a board decorated with battle maps and plans nearby. Pulling one map out, she spread it out on the table in front of the three Ronens.

"This is the battlefield near your homeland, as I remember it," she started, pointing at the centre of the map. All the three Ronens clustered around her for a better view.

"It hasn't changed," Avaron assured her, scrutinizing the map.

She gave a quick decisive nod. "Right. This is a ditch, I believe. We can position half of our archers there. With luck, the Shadow's army will think that the arrows are flying out of the ground."

"We can make it into a tunnel, right? If we get some warriors down there, we can probably build a tunnel and keep it standing by poles." Chester suggested.

"We'll need some time for that," she reminded the lion.

"So what?" Chester shrugged. "I can organize a troop and lead them there. I promise they will not be harmed," He looked challengingly at Miva. Finally she dipped her head.

"We can place the other half of the archers over here. It is a high platform," Romial suggested, pointing at the map.

The leader turned her attention back to the map. "Right. And we can ambush the camp from all sides. We can hide in the undergrowth here and beyond this river right here. Chester, can you get a tunnel dug here as well? It must connect to the other tunnel which you will dig in the ditch." Chester agreed.

"I will get another one also, all around this side of the camp," he said. "If you can afford a distraction, he will probably send his army towards that distraction. If we line up that tunnel with spears and spikes, and cover it with a net and soil, they will probably rush right into the pit, and will get speared." Chester suggested.

"Good idea. Then another group can sneak in from the other side and have them cornered. And if we manage to get some soldiers around the camp, to those low hanging trees, they can throw nets on the Shadow's army." Avaron said. After a moment's thought, he added, "If we take an army of dummies, we can place them in front of the camp. The Shadow will be fooled into thinking that the army is in the front while we attack from many places. They will probably think that we outnumber them much more vastly than we actually do."

"Excellent. We will send word to the other leaders from other tribes. We will discuss it further then." Miva put the map back where it was.

"Very well." The Ronens agreed, and left the leader's house.

"So back to training?" Romial sounded sceptical.

"Yes, of course." Avaron said, sounding tired as well.

"Maybe we should get some sleep. We are all tired," Chester pointed out. Without further argument, the three of them headed to their tents and climbed into their beds. All the three were asleep in a moment.

Chapter 13

"Do we have any flashlights?" Ron asked.

"Doesn't it look like we have any?" Carra snapped, pointing at the one Ruben clutched.

"I meant, don't we have more," Ron defended himself.

"Actually, I think I have some extra, if I could see what's in my bag," Max muttered. Ruben had switched off his flashlight by mistake, and couldn't figure out where the switch was.

"Give it to me, I can make it out," Tabitha said. Max handed the bag over to Carra, who held it in front of her bond. Tabitha stuck her head inside the bag, shoving aside other things. A muffled mew of joy reached them as she wriggled out of the bag, one flashlight in her jaws and pushing the rest out with her forepaws.

"Well done," Max said, smiling at where he thought the cat was. Tabitha placed her flashlight on the floor and switched it on with her paw. It shone brightly on the other five flashlights in front.

"Okay. I'll keep one, Amy, Josh, Zevyn, Iris and Lyke can take the others. Only two will be switched on at any given time. We don't want them all running out." Max instructed.

"What was said in that rhyme? I remember some steps?" Iris asked. May pulled out the riddles from where she'd stored them in her pocket. Checking it in the light of Iris's flashlight, she looked up.

"273 steps," she said. Iris' eyes widened. "I counted! There were 273 rungs on that ladder. We must be on the right path!"

"Good thinking," Max nodded approvingly. "We'd better move," Amy advised. The group inched forward.

They stopped abruptly as they felt water swishing around their feet. Max's flashlight flickered around the walls of what seemed to be a huge cavern with a tunnel leading away from both sides.

"Which way?" Lyke asked.

"Should I check it out?" Ruben offered. "Fine," Max agreed. "I'll come with you," Pete said, joining the hawk.

They waited for the two birds, their shoes and paws getting drenched in the shallow water. Tabitha jumped into Carra's arms, flicking the water from her paws crossly.

After what seemed to be an hour, but could just as well have been five minutes, the two birds emerged out of the darkness, Ruben's flashlight focussed on the water behind the group.

"What did you find?" Pal asked, before Ruben or Pete had a chance to open their beaks.

"It continues along for a long way. There is water on that side as well," Ruben said.

"There are those pointy rocks from both sides, and the water gets really deep," Pete added.

"It is not running water at first," Ruben started, but Pete cut him off, "It gets really fast later, and there's a waterfall too! It's damn huge, and really scary. There's absolutely no way you can go that way."

"Then this way it is," Max said firmly. They trudged onwards, Pal rushing forward, playing in the water. After a while, the water deepened. May had to carry Snowflake as the water reached a little above their knees. Pal enjoyed the most, as the water reached to his shoulders, and he splashed and swam, almost tripping all of them more than once.

Pretty soon, stalagmites and stalactites showed up everywhere, even in the middle of the river. The group had to navigate their way slowly, being careful not to trip over an underwater or bang their head on an overhanging living rock.

"Aagh!" Zevyn screamed. Everyone whirled around to find her resurfacing from the water.

"What happened?" Lyke was at his sister's side in an instant. He helped the drenched girl stand up.

"I tripped over this stupid rock!" she fumed. Lyke tried to calm his short-tempered sister, so that they could move on. After a short while of travelling, Ron let out a cry of excitement.

"Guys, I found something!" Pal ran over to his bond's side, his tail wagging.

"Look! There's a secret panel over here!" Ron said, fingering a crack running down the wall.

"You're right! Should I open it?" Carra asked her mother.

Amy nodded, and her daughter felt along the cracks, trying to figure out where the door was. She traced the crack in a huge square, and pushed in the centre. It creaked, but didn't open.

She looked at the others for help, and they all pushed together. It finally opened with an echoing *boom,* and a gaping hole yawned in front of them. Max shone his flashlight into the darkness. The beam illuminated a structure made of wood.

"What is that?" Tabitha asked, peering in.

"Is that the ferry?" Snowflake asked.

"Yes! It must be!" Lyke cried.

"It looks more like a ship," Amy frowned.

"I'll go check it out," Josh said, and climbed in as if the adults had already given him permission. He switched on his flashlight and shone it on the small ferry. Ron followed him, but the rest stayed where they were.

"It is a ship, but a tiny one. And it seems to be creaky."

The two boys took their own time to check the whole ship over. It was small, and most of the paint had faded away, leaving patches of gloomy red.

"Is it fine?" Snowflake asked, her voice echoing strangely.

"Yeah, I think so. But I don't know if we have to push it into that tunnel or go this way. Max, can you help?" Josh called back.

"I'm coming." Max climbed into the tunnel with the ship. He pushed past the boys and checked out the tunnel. Turning around, he asked, "May, what was the riddle about?"

The girl took out the pieces of paper she had kept in her pocket. She read them out in the light of Ruben's flashlight.

"Hmm," Amy said as May finished. "We should climb up the ship, that's for sure. Maybe there's a clue up there."

Ruben flew up and quickly checked around for any booby traps, just in case. When he gave the 'all clear' signal, the group boarded, one by one. But their unexpected weight made the ship shift its position, and it started rolling down the tunnel, leaving behind a startled Josh and Lyke, who were yet to board. They yelped in astonishment and gave chase. The ship, however, had different plans. It started gaining momentum as the tunnel sloped downwards.

The two boys could hear the calls and screams of those on board as they fell back further and further. They stopped, panting.

"Now what do we do?" Josh asked despairingly. He sank down in disappointment and dismay. "We can still go down the tunnel. Ruben might come back for us," Lyke suggested hopefully. "How in the world can he possibly do that? That ship was going way too fast for a cheetah to cope with, let alone a hawk! It was probably going at like, what, five thousand metres a second? Ruben can never outpace that! It will take too damn long to reach the ship with *one* of us, let alone two!" Josh exploded. He was angrier than he had ever been. It seemed to him that he was facing failure smack in the face, after he had tried so hard.

Lyke tried to be positive, forcing Josh to jog along the tunnel, but he was failing miserably and his hopes were dying. They trotted down the dark tunnel. Thankfully, both had fully functioning flashlights. The tunnel was gloomy and dark, and the two were glad they had each other's company.

Suddenly, another beam of light found their faces. Both held their hands in front of their eyes, squinting to see through the glare. A happy screech welcomed them. In a mighty thunder, Ruben the hawk swooped down to the rescue.

Lyke punched Josh in an I-told-you-so manner. Josh felt his face grow hot. "I hoped I was wrong too," he muttered sheepishly. Ruben descended, switching off his flashlight and holding it in his beak before alighting.

"It is some distance to the ship. You both will walk," Ruben said, without giving them a chance to speak.

"What do you mean?" Lyke asked.

"I will-"

"Where is the ship?" Josh asked.

"It is-"

"What happened to the others?"

"They are-"

"Is everybody okay?"

"Be quiet! The others are all fine. It is some distance away, the ship, I mean. You are going to walk. We will have rests in between," he added, glaring at Josh who was opening his mouth to protest. He shut it quickly.

"Come on then," Ruben said, flapping his wings. He rose to the air and led the boys, forcing them to a brisk trot.

They walked on for a long time.

"How did the ship stop?" Josh asked.

"It crashed into another ship."

"What?"

"Yes. You will see for yourself soon. Now sit down. You can rest for some time."

The two boys sank to the floor in relief, trying to ease the pain in their legs. No sooner had they sat down, though, than an echoing bark reached them.

"Pal!" Josh cried, though he made no move to get up.

"Josh, Lyke. I'm here," Pal called back. Now they could hear his panting and the patter of his paw steps on the rock floor. Finally he emerged from the gloom, a flashlight in his mouth.

"The others were wondering where you three were. So they sent me."

"We will move now," Ruben said firmly. Lyke sighed as he stood wearily. Josh had more energy than his friend, even though he was tired. They resumed their walk, making good time. Pal had rested for a couple of minutes, and he padded behind them. They reached the ship eventually, just as the group were making preparations to send Tabitha as well.

When Ruben led the two boys to where the ship was, they could do nothing but gape at the sight they saw. The ship which the others had ridden was in pieces, completely broken. Wooden pieces lay scattered everywhere. In front of the mauled ship was another one, but magnificent. It was wooden, but painted to shine a lustrous gold, with carved designs in red and blue and green. The mast was painted black, but neither ship had any sail. Along the sides, the name *Beautiful Storm* was painted in black.

"Wow," Josh breathed. Lyke just stood there, gaping.

"Come on up!" A voice called. The two tore their gazes from the ship and saw Amy waving at them. "There's a ladder on that side."

They went round the side of the ship and saw a rope ladder dangling from the side. They glanced at each other and made a run for it. They both grabbed the sides of the ladder together, just in case even this ship left without them. Josh kept a tight grip on the ladder and then followed Lyke who had pushed past and climbed up.

As they reached the top, the ship groaned and moved an inch. A frightened yelp came from down as Pal scrabbled to the ladder, placing his paws clumsily on the rope to get up. With Ruben's help, the dog climbed the swaying ladder. A waiting Josh and Ron pulled Pal up and Ruben landed beside them. By then the ship had picked up speed and was sailing down the tunnel at full pelt.

May and Iris peered over the side. The ship was suddenly on swirling black water. As May looked closer, tiny bubbles popped at the surface, and a giant monster was suddenly inches from her face. Screaming, she fell back.

"What happened?" Amy asked, rushing over.

"A monster!" Iris gasped, eyes wide with fear. "In the water. It jumped out."'

"Carra, tie a flashlight to the front of the ship," Max ordered. "Pete, tie one on the rear end. We'll take turns on the look-out. Zevyn, climb up the main mast and keep a look-out there." Zevyn, Pete and Carra rushed to their allotted places. Max shone his flashlight on the roof of the cave. A hundred eyes glinted in the light and disappeared a second before a hurricane of flapping wings dove towards the ship.

They instinctively ducked, and the flapping creatures sailed onwards. Zevyn shone her flashlight on the one beast which was still on deck. The beam of light fell on a brown creature with giant black eyes and fangs. It looked pretty much like a monkey, except for its tail, which was extremely long and suddenly fanned open, covering its face.

Ron screamed. Pal barked loudly, and the creature shied away, covering its ears with its paws.

"What is that thing?" Zevyn shrieked.

"Calm down!" Max called out, and inched forward slowly towards the monster. It started whimpering, and curled into a perfect brown furry ball. He reached out slowly and touched it with a finger. He started stroking it, and it uncurled itself inch by inch, and lowered its tail to look at Max. He smiled at it and it crept forward. The black in its eyes shrunk like a cat's, revealing purple eyes.

"It's cute," May whispered, stroking the creature, which promptly climbed into her lap and grinned, folding back its fangs.

"Foldable fangs?" she whispered. It spread its tail again, which revealed tiny spikes at the end. Iris reached out to touch the spikes, but the creature drew its tail back, looking annoyed.

"I think the spikes are poisonous," May interpreted the animal's expression. The monkey like face spread into a grin.

"Woah! It understands you!" Carra laughed. It started prancing around, unfurling its wings, a goofy laugh on its face. A huge splash brought them all running to one side of a ship. A gigantic horn vanished into the dark water.

"What in the world?" Ron exclaimed.

"This place definitely has some weird creatures." Tabitha jumped onto the wooden side and leaned over.

"Careful," Amy cautioned. The cat leaped back onto the deck.

"Come away," Max called. Telling May and Amy to check the stock of food, he ordered the rest to go down to the cabins and check them out.

As May settled down with a bag, she wondered what to name the animal on her shoulder.

"How about Violet?" May asked suddenly. "What, dear?" Amy asked, looking up. "For her," the girl pointed to the chattering animal. "Violet after her eyes," she explained.

"That's a good name," Amy smiled, and continued unpacking their food. Violet jumped around, as if approving her name. May turned back to her work and was shocked to find the bag empty.

"Is that all?" she asked, eyes wide. Amy checked again. "We're dangerously low," she muttered.

"Max!" she called. He turned around. "We got all the food here. We're probably going to starve."

"That can't possibly be all!" Max exclaimed. There were three cans of tinned food, two packs of chips and some sandwiches. Max groaned.

"What's up?" Carra asked from the front of the ship. She glanced at the food lying on the deck. "Where's the rest of it?"

"That's all there is," Amy said sadly.

"Maybe we can find something 'round here."

Amy shrugged. Violet widened her eyes and danced around waving frantically. They looked at where she was pointing and saw a faint outline.

"Land! There's land up ahead! I can see it!" Zevyn called out shrilly.

"Clever girl!" May smiled, picking up Violet.

Meanwhile, down in the cabins, Tabitha and Pal had smelled something and had led their group to it.

"What is it?" Ron asked for the third time. "I can't make out." Pal sniffed the air some more before following the trail. "It kind of smells like books and bombs rolled in one."

"Okaay." Ron looked around nervously.

Tabitha picked up a stronger scent and followed it to a table. She went over to the side and vanished!

"T-Tabitha?" Ron called. No reply.

Lyke strode to where the cat had been and inspected it. "She didn't vanish, Ron. She went through this hole here." Lyke pointed to a hole in the wall. Without further hesitation, Lyke disappeared through it too. Exchanging worried glances, Ron and his bond crawled through the hole.

Chapter 14

Josh emptied the dusty bag he had found in a compartment. The cabin they were searching was full of bags and 'something like suitcases', according to Josh.

"Same as last. Bits of metal and scrap. Nothing more," he announced. Iris sighed. "I do not think that there is anything useful here. Where is Snow?"

"I'm here." A dusty bunny popped out from behind a chair. She shook out her fur. "There's nothing but cardboard back there."

"I doubt there is anything more we can do here," Ruben announced, unfurling his wings. His wings brushed against a set of boxes balancing precariously on top of each other. The boxes tumbled down from the table they were on, burying Snowflake underneath. The bunny shook the boxes off grumpily and looked at the others. They were all staring at what had been underneath the boxes.

"It can't be!" Josh cried. On the table was a glass case. Inside the case, a miniature Ron, Lyke, Pal and Tabitha were pounding the glass, screaming. They stopped, eyes wide in amazement when the saw the humungous Josh looming over the glass.

"What in the world happened?" Snowflake whispered. Iris leaned forward, touching the glass case with a finger. Pal placed his paw on the same spot on his side. Iris' finger was a bit bigger than Pal's paw.

"Fetch Max," she ordered. Ruben shot out of the room and flew up. As he flew out, May picked up the monkey creature and smiled, "Clever girl."

"Max!" he screeched. The man turned around, surprised. "What is it?" he asked, frowning at the hawk's worried expression.

"Come and see for yourself." Ruben led Max down to the cabin, Zevyn and Carra following. They entered the cabin, bewildered expressions on their faces. Max gasped when he saw his son in the glass case. Zevyn let out a strangled cry, while Carra stared at her bond in her horror.

"What the hell happened?" Carra asked softly, not able to believe what she saw.

"Right. How did you end up here?" Max asked Ron. The tiny boy spoke, but it was very soft, and no-one could hear it. Max sighed and looked down at his feet. A knocking sound made him look up. Ron was beckoning him closer. Max placed his ear on the glass, and Ron related their story in his loudest voice.

Max nodded. He turned to the others. "Ron says that Tabitha and Pal found a scent trail and followed it. There was a table behind which the smell was coming from, and these four followed it there. There was an opening there, I believe, and they crawled through. But there was a hole on the other side, and they fell through and ended up here. I don't know what to do now." Max looked more worried than he had ever been.

"Can't they go back the way they came?" Zevyn glanced down at her brother. He shrugged. Turning around, he knocked the glass on the other side from which they popped through.

A sudden *crack* and the glass fell open. Lyke looked at it in shock. Ron ran to his side, his bond and Tabitha following. The two tiny boys looked at their giant comrades. What should they do?

Pal pattered up to the side and peeped down. There was floor under it, not a hole. "Should we jump? What if there's an invisible portal and we'll go back to our proper size?" he asked. Lyke shrugged.

"I think we should try it," Tabitha said, determined. "If it doesn't work, we'll just fall down right? What's the harm? We could ask them to put something soft, just in case."

Ron nodded. "We should try it." Lyke went to the opposite glass and shouted to Zevyn and told her their plans. She nodded, worried, and relayed the message to the others. They started searching, while Snowflake went up to call the others down. Soon, Carra had found a soft Styrofoam sheet and pulled it in front of the open glass.

Nodding gratefully at the girl, Lyke prepared himself. The others watched tersely. He took a deep breath, made a running start, and jumped. Midway down to the ground, he disappeared.

"Lyke?" Ron called anxiously. Snowflake suddenly turned around, pricking her ears. Thudding of footsteps? How? They were all in this room! Suddenly, Lyke burst through the door, his normal size.

"Lykenzar!" Zevyn cried, hugging her brother.

"It works!" Max laughed. They turned back to the glass. Ron was already running. He leaped, disappeared. Pal and Tabitha jumped together, and vanished. Moments later, they were all in the room, talking, laughing and crying all at once.

Celebrating, they went to the deck. As soon as they reached, they fell to their knees. The ship groaned and hit something hard again, and stopped shaking. When they saw what the ship had hit, they were all on their feet in an instant and climbing off it. They had reached the land.

Chapter 15

"This is our plan. Does anybody object or have a question or opinion?" the Streo leader asked the council. Avaron looked around. Nobody objected. They had called a meeting of all the leaders they knew to form an alliance against The Shadow.

"I think we could use some of our people for a tactical advantage." A young leader stood up.

"Well, enlighten us," Romial said impatiently.

He took out the battle map and explained his view. Soon, there were smiles on everyone's faces, and they were all nodding in agreement.

"That's a good plan. You'll make a very intelligent ruler soon," Avaron congratulated him. He smiled shyly and sat down again. Miva concluded that the meeting was over, and all the leaders dispersed.

"We'd better get back to training now," Avaron decided, and the three Ronens went to the training centre. Word had already spread about the new plan, and the troops were undergoing the slightly different training.

They had shifted base to a much bigger clearing which could accommodate all the ally's troops. Now the clearing was completely packed, with creatures of every shape and size training and battling in various ways.

A legion of winged creatures rose to the air at a sharp call. They were the Veria. They avoided mock arrows, twisting and manoeuvring in the sky easily, pausing to spit fire of their own. Down below, Chester was leading a group of huge handed troll-like figures, the Musker, to dig the tunnels. Storin, king of the Xasfi, strode over to Avaron. The Xasfi were hairy two headed beasts with spikes down their backs, known for using their strong tails for constricting their enemies.

"Avaron, tomorrow isss Xassshi day. We celebrate it imppportantly. Asss your equal, I am asssking your permissssion for celebrasssion," he hissed in a strange accent. Avaron agreed, assuring Storin that he would discuss with the other leaders and notify the king later. Storin went back to training his people, his extra long tail snaking around the path.

Avaron decided to get the job over with and called all the leaders for a meeting. When they joined him, he informed them of Storin's request. Agreeing that the soldiers needed a feast, they all agreed, and sent word to the cooks of all species.

The Xasfi did excellent in the training after the feast was announced. Avaron realized that they had been looking forward for this for so long, and it motivated them to train much better. Even the others performed better than they used to.

As night fell, they winded up and started setting up the camps. They built a huge fire in the middle and positioned the camps in a ring around it, with the exception of the Tsist, who preferred to sleep in the high branches of the trees.

While Avaron set up his tent with Romial, he wondered where his bond was. Chester had not returned yet, and Avaron, for the first time, worried if his bond could manage the Musker. He looked up, scanning the surroundings, when suddenly, Chester's illuminated form appeared on the crest of a slope. He ran down with the Musker on his tail. All of them were baked in earth, and sand and grit flew off them as they entered the clearing.

Miva hurried out of her tent, closely followed by the others. "What is the news?"

“We dug a tunnel and shored it up. The roof seems to be a little unstable, but tomorrow, we can fix it. Hopefully, there will be no cave-ins.”

Miva and the others nodded. “Well done,” Avaron congratulated. The lion shook out his fur, sending grit and soil flying. Avaron looked up. Quirodon was already in the sky, while Satiro peeked out from behind distant mountains.

The Ronen leader returned to his tent with his bond and Romial. The next day, a Veria and Hikint had been sent as messengers to the Streo campsite. Chester led the Musker out again, all of them determined. Some pulled carts full of timber and tools to shore up the tunnels, while others carried sacks of food for lunch. The feast was to be for dinner.

A drum started beating and the training started for the day. The Veria dove and swooped in the air with screeches, avoiding arrows from the best professional Streos, and when given the chance, the armoured beasts returned fire with fire. Avaron watched the way they moved gracefully through the air even with the metal protection they were supposed to wear against the arrows.

The Tsist crept silently through the trees, not making a sound. Not even a leaf stirred to give away their presence. Below the eaves of the trees, several Hikints and Xasfi looked above them suspiciously, trying to figure out where their attackers were hiding. Even from his vantage point of view above the hill, where he could see through the branches clearly, Avaron could not point out where the Tsist lurked. A branch swished, and the Tsist dropped on the troops below. Their scaly jade skin was a blur as they pushed the defender’s heads to the grounds with their four clawed hands. The defenders fought back fiercely, managing to throw off some Tsist. The Hikints jabbed the Tsist with sticks, while the Xasfi spat and coiled their lengthy tails around their waists.

Romial was sparring with a couple of Makix, who were just as skilled as the Ronen, with their horned heads and huge lower canines, which jutted out of their jaw as deadly tusks. Their sheer size and protective, hard scales, added with their razor-sharp claws, made them a deadly enemy. They were short tempered, not very unlike the Musker, which made both of them all the more dangerous. The Hikints, Streos and Veria, on the other hand, were very long tempered, but fought with fatal precision. The Xasfi and Tsist fought on their instincts, and played with their enemies before moving in for the kill.

Avaron gazed at the scene once more, and climbed down the hill. He knew he should be training, but he didn't feel like it. He was too preoccupied in his thoughts to notice Romial backing away in defeat from the two Makix. Romial turned around and just managed to avoid crashing into his leader.

"Avaron? What is wrong?" he asked. The Ronen leader turned around with a start. He shook his head. "Nothing, my friend. I was just thinking about Iris and the others."

"Why do you not try battling with them?" Romial nodded towards the two Makix. "You will forget your troubles for a while." He led his leader towards the two warriors and they stood, ready to attack. The Makix charged, heads lowered. The two Ronens yelled a battle cry and raised their swords, ready to meet their attackers. The Makix swerved aside at the last instant, but the Ronens swerved around, fast as a snake, and clashed their swords against the sharp tusks. The Ronens seemed to be gaining ground, but one Makix yanked his head up, sending a surprised Avaron flying. He hadn't expected the opponent to be that strong! Defeating Romial then was easy, and the two Ronens graciously accepted defeat.

"Lesson learned number one; never underestimate your enemy," Avaron muttered, rubbing his arm. He had landed awkwardly on it when he was thrown away. Now the Makix walked up to him, bowing, apologized profusely. Avaron forgave him readily with a smile, and praised him for his skills.

The day wore on, and as night approached, everyone ceased fighting as they eagerly waited for the feast. The moons rose, and everything was set up. Laughing, talking and drinking, the feast continued for a better part of the night, and even the moons seemed to be enjoying themselves, shining brightly, illuminating the whole clearing.

Chapter 16

"Is this stuff *edible?*" Zevyn frowned at the brown fruit she held in her hands. "It looks like it could kill you," Josh agreed. Amy shrugged and threw it away. Iris followed her action.

"Mom!" Carra called from further inland. Amy turned her attention on her daughter. Carra was pointing at something in the floor. It was an intricately carved stone slab. A little pushing revealed a key under it.

"Now what the hell is this for?" Josh muttered, picking it up. It was silver, with bits of red and green and blue stones. Tabitha suddenly let out a gasp of surprise. There was a drawing in the stone slab, one which showed the key in a door made of blue gems.

"Now that's surprising," Amy commented. Pete sat on the carving, studying it closely. "There's somebody with an elephant head here. Looks familiar."

"That's a Hindu god!" Amy exclaimed, brushing Pete off the slab. He flew off, squawking indignantly. She called Max, who had taken Ron, Pal, Lyke, May and Snowflake to forage for more supplies. He came instantly, the rest of his group crowding behind him.

She showed him the slab and the key. "There are carvings of some Hindu gods too. I studied Indian legends when I was younger. There's Ganapati, and that one's Hanuman. That's Krishna, Vishnu and Shiva. And that one, which is holding the instrument, is Saraswati." She turned the slab over, which revealed a lot more figures.

"It shows a door. Where could that be?" Ruben asked thoughtfully. "It's probably in a temple. Some ancient one from around," Snowflake suggested. "Why?" Pal asked, shaking out his fur for no reason. "There are god's carvings here." Snowflake nodded at the stone slab. "I think it's pretty obvious that gods are found in temples, so probably the door's there as well."

"That's a good observation," Max noted. May smiled at her bond, and Violet chattered, prancing around like a monkey.

"Where do you think a temple would be over here? And who would have constructed it?" Lyke wondered. "The same people who made the opening in Hampi, and the same people who probably built that ship."

As Josh said that, everyone remembered those events. It seemed like a lifetime ago to them.

"So now to find this temple and the door, then the lotus and get back to Imagneus," Iris announced. "What about food?" Ron's stomach grumbled.

"Fine, food first, temple later." After finding some edible fruits, they went back to the temple carving, in case they'd missed a clue. They found a small engraving on the other side of the slab. It showed an 'Om' symbol next to a huge banyan tree, with a lake on the other side.

"I guess that 'Om' represents the temple, and it's next to a banyan tree, which is next to a lake." Zevyn squinted at the slab. "Let's go!"

They set off, Ruben and Pete scouting ahead for any sign of the lake. They soon glided down to join the group. "We can see it up ahead," Pete reported. "Just follow us."

Soon, they reached the shore of a big, crystal clear lake, which had an island in the middle. Ruben and Pete flew off to find the banyan tree, while the rest decided to sit down and chat. A swoosh of wings announced the arrival of the two birds.

"The banyan tree and the temple are on the island. We saw both of them," Pete reported. "How do we cross the lake?" Ron asked, looking at the expanse of water that separated them from the temple. Ruben shook his head. "There does not seem to be any kind of bridge as far as I can see."

"Can you check again?"

Pete and Ruben rose into the air once more, gliding high above. They landed next to the others after some time.

"There's a fallen tree," Pete said. "It looks slippery. You will have to cross carefully." They followed the two birds to the tree. It was a tall oak tree. The bark was withering, and the water lapped at its bottom. Max decided to go first, and inched along the tree trunk, almost falling over twice. As he neared the end, he grasped the branches for support, and made it across safely. May followed, with Snowflake at her heels. Pretty soon, everyone had made it across, except for Pal, who had fallen over in the middle and was now swimming towards the island.

Before Pal even reached the shore, everybody went to the temple, not wanting to get drenched by one of his fur-shakes. They found the temple pretty quick. It was made of stone and had ivy vines growing along the sides with moss at the base. It had engravings all around which had withered away, but they could make out a very large 'Om' symbol at the very front.

The door was a huge slab of stone with a tiny keyhole in the centre. Fishing out the key from his pocket, Max slid it into the hole and turned. A click indicated that the door was unlocked, and it swung open on rusty hinges.

"Do we go inside?" Zevyn asked, glancing eagerly at the cobweb filled doorway of the temple. Max nodded, and led the way inside, grabbing the torchlight from his bag and switching it on. A loud roar stopped them in their tracks.

"Thunder!" Amy called from outside. Ron let out a loud sigh of relief. The patter of rain started, which turned into a storm in no time at all. The sound of the raindrops on the temple walls sounded eerie from inside, seeming to magnify itself when it echoed through the walls.

Iris suddenly stopped, frozen to her spot, staring at a sideway, causing Carra to bump into her. "Hey, what's wrong? Move-" her words froze on her tongue as she saw what Iris was looking at.

Chapter 17

"Run," Iris breathed, but neither could move. The giant serpent slithered closer, its tongue flicking out. The others turned around.

"Hey, what's the hold up?" Amy called from the front. The serpent had transfixed them with its amber gaze, not letting them move a muscle. Ron grabbed his cousin's hand, about to pull her forward when he saw the giant snake. He screamed and bolted, not looking back.

"Snake! Snake!" he shrieked in everyone's confused faces. Josh joined Iris and Carra. The serpent was coming closer, closer slowly, flicking its tongue in and out, its fiery eyes not once leaving the two girls. Josh gave one glance at the serpent, and stood stock-still.

The serpent rounded the corner and fixed the rest of the group with its fiery eyes. Everyone's eyes widened visibly, but they too, could not move.

"Ssso you are the lotusss ssseekersss," it hissed, coiling itself around the terrified group. "Don't fear me, I only wisshh you well." Nobody made a sound. The snake let out a huge breath through its nostrils, a sigh. It uncoiled itself from them and drew back a little.

"I am going to test you a little, then we sshall have introducctionsss." The serpent seemed to smirk. "We'll play a little game firssst. Come." With that, it slithered away, the tip of its tail coiling around the group, forcing them to a slow trot.

They reached a big room, which seemed impossible since the temple seemed so small from outside. The snake stopped and fixed its amber gaze on them again.

"Reach that," it pointed at a shiny object stuck in the ceiling, "without getting eaten. The birds should stay on the ground." It disappeared, leaving the group very confused. "Without getting eaten?" Ron asked, frowning.

"That's easy. Violet can get it for us, while we protect her," May said. Violet seemed to agree, and her little face turned to a grin. The creature scampered to the nearest wall and began to climb very swiftly.

The wall behind them shifted, and many huge spiders rushed out of the crevice. Ron shrieked, no surprise. The brown creatures scurried towards the group, jaws drooling. A couple veered off to the side to intercept a screeching Violet.

"How the hell are we supposed to fight them? We don't have any weapons!" Josh protested. As if on cue, a bunch of weapons landed with a *thump* beyond the mega-spiders.

"Just great," Carra muttered. "Pete, Ruben!" Max ordered. "The snake said they have to stay on the ground!" Amy cried. "They are not getting the weapons," Iris said, catching on. "They are going to distract the spiders."

The two birds spread their wings, catching the spiders' attention. Most of them stepped on each other to surround the birds. "Zevyn, now!" Lyke bent over. Zevyn jumped on her brother's back, easily catapulting over the remaining spider's heads, and landed right next to the weapons. She quickly dealt them out, throwing them over the mega-spiders. A couple of swords, twin blades, a double-headed battle axe, three rapiers, a bow and a quiver full of arrows landed right next to Ron. Zevyn had kept a sword for herself, and slicing off the head of a spider, she pushed off its back and landed on her feet beside her brother.

Tabitha and Iris broke ranks to help Violet. They took out the two spiders which were chasing Violet, and she continued scaling the wall.

"Violet! We can't hold them off for long!" May yelled, shooting an arrow from the bow. The monkey creature nodded in understanding and sped up. She swung herself up the last couple metres and grabbed the shiny object. The spiders stopped in their tracks and seemed to literally melt into the floor. The dead bodies disintegrated into sand, which vanished after a moment.

Violet scampered down the wall, holding out the object. Amy took it from the creature, and held it to the light from a skylight, gasping.

"It's a... lotus!"

Chapter 18

"Congratulationsss."

The serpent emerged out of thin air.

"The lotus! This is the one!" Iris exclaimed, her eyes lighting up. The snake's face contorted into a weird smirk. "You figured it out, I sssssee."

"Come on! We have to get back now!" Pete called, spreading his wings, ready to take flight.

"Not ssso fassst, birdie," the snake hissed, amusement in its tone. "What do you mean?" Ron cried.

"You're the guardian," Max realized. "The guardian of the lotus."

"Well done. You realizzzed."

"Let us go! The Ronens will die if we don't get there in time!"

"And when, exactly, isss 'in time'?"

"What the hell? We have to go back *now* or the Shadow guy will kill everyone!"

"But I never sssaid that I will let you go asss sssoon ass you get the lotusss."

"You tricked us!"

"Fraud!"

"Me? I never promised anything," the snake mocked innocently. Iris glared fiercely at the Lotus Guardian.

"Oh, I've had enough of this!" Zevyn spat and marched forward, her blade in hand. She catapulted into the air, and, holding her blade forward, drove it into the snake. Or at least, that's what she expected to happen. Instead, while she was still in the air, the blade disintegrated into sand. Zevyn was so surprised she lost balance but managed to land on her feet in front of the serpent. The other weapons had become miniature sand dunes as well.

"Hey, umm, Lotus?" Ron raised his hand as if to ask a question. The snake turned its piercing eyes on Ron. "Umm, I can call you Lotus, right? 'Cause Gaurdian of the Lotus is such a long name?" he said, more like a question. The serpent was staring at the boy in shock.

"He's distracting it! Iris, Lyke, Zevyn, Ruben, you get back to Imagneus as fast as you can. We'll try to follow. Save the Ronens!" Max whispered urgently. The Lotus Guardian's gaze was still locked on Ron.

"NO! The Lotus Guardian or Guardian of the Lotus is and always will be my name. You have no right to tamper with such an honourable name," it hissed angrily.

"Oh! I'm so s-sorry, Lotus Guardian. But d-do you mind if I ask a few questions?" Ron stammered. "Go on," the snake said with a nod of its head. All the while, Ruben, Iris, Lyke and Zevyn were slowly inching towards the entrance.

"Ummm, so yeah, like, what's your real name? I mean, you got your name when you were hired right?"

"Hired?"

"Yeah, like when you signed up for this job. You didn't start guarding the lotus as soon as you were born right?"

"You mean you want my life history?" The snake gazed at Ron with hopeful eyes.

"Umm, yeah, something like that if you don't mind."

The snake let out a hiss of delight, and curled up comfortably, wrapping its tail around itself. With its back to the entrance of the room, it didn't notice the disappearance of two girls, a boy and a hawk.

"Settle down, boy. It's a long story."

"And it's a long night, isn't it?" Max muttered, standing next to his son.

"Is it night? I thought it was afternoon," Josh grumbled. They all sat down.

"I was born as the runt of the batch," the snake started melodramatically. May raised an eyebrow, and Josh rolled his eyes. "My siblings bullied me, and my mother didn't stop them. I fought back of course, but they were bigger, and they would try and put me in place. My mother abandoned me soon, and left me to survive on my own." The serpent paused for a breath.

"But I learnt the trickeries of the world and survived on my own. I became stronger everyday and learnt to give what I had to survive. There was this time when a fox tried to eat me. Hah! It got a nasty surprise. It underestimated me, like everyone else." The Lotus Guardian put on a scowl.

Everyone blocked out the drone of the snake's voice as it rambled on about its twisted life. After re-accounting about two score incidents, the Guardian finally got to the point where it became the Guardian.

"And the previous Guardian gave me the post with those exact words." Ron yawned loudly. Josh's head slumped on Pal, and Carra blinked repeatedly to fight off her drowsiness. The snake hissed at them, irritated.

"Whoa! I'm awake, I'm awake," Ron held up his hands. Only Josh snored on, undeterred. The Lotus Guardian narrowed its eyes at the sleeping boy.

"Hey, um, Lotus Guardian, I forgot your real name again," Snowflake said immediately. The snake turned its head. Amy flashed the rabbit a grateful glance before fiercely waking Josh up.

"My name, as I told you three times already, is-"

The serpent was interrupted by Josh's yawn, which equalled the sound of a flight taking off.

"Enjoyed your dream?" It asked Josh sarcastically. "Oh, yeah." Josh nodded. "Are you going to let us go now?" Pete asked. The Lotus Guardian glared at him with its fiery gaze.

"No."

Chapter 19

"Come quickly!" Ruben called, flying ahead. Lyke, Iris and Zevyn ran behind the hawk, stumbling over the undergrowth in their haste. They had crossed the log from the island, and were now racing across the forest on the other shore.

Ruben slowed down as he reached the ship. The three children halted panting for breath.

"So how do we get back now?" Lyke asked, once they had rested for a few moments. Iris eyed the lotus, staring at it fiercely as if sheer determination will automatically transport them back. It happened much differently though.

Zevyn and Ruben went down to the ship to check out if there was anything useful. As they groped around, Zevyn chanced upon the glass box in which her miniature brother had been trapped. Grabbing it, the girl tried to walk out, almost falling over due to its weight. Ruben offered to help, which she gratefully accepted. They hauled it over to where Lyke and Iris were waiting. They managed to place it as gently as they could; in this case, with a loud *thud* that could have scared off birds from trees, had there been birds or trees so close to the shore.

"Maybe you should learn to place things more softly," Lyke suggested, wincing visibly when his sister dropped the box.

"Then maybe you could have been of some help, instead of dreaming around!" the shorter girl snapped. Lyke held up his hands, surrendering, while Zevyn smirked.

Iris wandered around the glass box, running her hands over it. She stopped suddenly, fingering one side. "Look at this. I think there is something here," she beckoned to the others. Zevyn felt the side of the glass box. "You're right." she nodded. "There's something written here." She traced the letters. "It's in Sanskrit."

"Can you read it?" Ruben asked hopefully. The girl nodded, flipping back her hair and kneeling down.

She muttered something to herself, then looked up. "It's the way to get back," she announced, grinning. "Really? What do we do?" Lyke asked, almost jumping up and down in excitement. His hair shimmered with lightning, and he stopped, puzzled.

"I thought Minkin took away our special powers," he mumbled. Zevyn's eyes grew wide as her ears became cat-like, and her green wings grew back.

"What in the world is going on?" Lyke asked, his newly grown tail dragging on the ground.

"We are right next to the portal. Maybe that is why you are changing back to normal," Ruben suggested. Zevyn laughed. "I don't care, I got my wings back!"

"We had better go back as soon as we can," Iris warned. "Yeah," Zevyn agreed, and translated the words on the box. "We have to walk through the box," she started. Iris frowned. "How do we do that?" The shorter girl shrugged. "It just says so. After we fix the lotus there," she pointed to a little dent on the box, "And we'll be back on Imagneus."

"But what about the others?" Ruben asked. "We'll probably have to ask Avaron to get them back after the war. But till then, I'm afraid they're out of action."

"You mean, we just leave them there with that horrible snake?" Lyke asked, shocked. "There's no other way, Lykenzar." Zevyn's huge cat eyes showed that she was feeling miserable about leaving them behind.

"We cannot just do that!" Iris exclaimed, horrified. "All of them knew that all of us couldn't escape. That's why Ron distracted that snake, didn't he? We will find a way to get them back," Zevyn's eyes filled with determination.

"Come on then," Lyke said, hesitantly taking the lotus from Iris. He found the groove and slowly pushed the lotus into place. Nothing happened.

"And now we're supposed to just walk through?" He asked sarcastically. "What, don't you believe your own sister?" Zevyn shot back. With a glare, she stormed through the box, which provided no resistance at all. The moment she was completely inside, she vanished into thin air.

Lyke wasted no time in following his sibling. Iris exchanged a glance with her bond. "Father told us that he needs the lotus to defeat the Shadow. How are we going to get it if we need it to get back?" Iris asked, frowning.

"Maybe it was like a switch. You need to place it once, and the portal will remain open for some time, so you can remove it."

Iris nodded. "Maybe you are right. Good thinking." She removed the lotus from its place and walked in. She disappeared with the lotus. Ruben nodded in satisfaction and followed.

❋ ❋ ❋

The four found themselves in an unfamiliar landscape.

"Where did we end up?" Lyke asked, swishing his tail. They couldn't see; it was completely dark. None of the three moons were visible, either they hadn't risen, or they were blocked.

"Weird," Zevyn muttered. She could see just fine, due to her cat eyes.

Lyke closed his eyes, and a few seconds later, several bolts of lightning rose from his hands, formed a single sphere of light, and lit up their surroundings.

They were completely surrounded by trees and bushes, with no way through. Ruben tried to fly up, but the branches of the trees crowded above them, blocking any way of flying.

They started moving forward, pushing through the undergrowth. Ruben growled as twigs and leaves and dirt stuck on to his feathers. Zevyn seemed uncomfortable to walk now that she got her wings back, but she didn't complain.

The lightning sphere formed dancing shadows all along their path, leading them to believe that there was twice the number of obstacles on the ground than there actually was. They kept trying to avoid imaginary stones and ended up tripping over real ones.

"Can't you make your sphere brighter?" Iris snapped when she stumbled for the infinitieth time. Zevyn, the only one who hadn't tripped even once due to her special sight, replied. "It has been some time since he used his lightning. He needs time to get used to it, and energy too. If he makes it brighter, he'll lose all his energy, and we'll have to carry him." She ended with a shudder. "I *definitely* do not want that."

Lyke laughed, and that merry sound seemed very out of place in the dark forest. Yet, it lightened their mood slightly. Suddenly, Lyke stopped, his tail swishing from side to side slowly. His hair buzzed with electricity as he motioned the others to stay where they were. Zevyn inched closer though, pricking her ears in an attempt to hear better. Lyke moved aside to let his sister pass.

"What is it?" Ruben whispered from the back. "Something's there," Zevyn whispered back, flattening her ears. Suddenly something exploded from the bushes ahead, and Zevyn leaped forward to meet it. They crashed mid-air, and grappled with each other. The other creature had jade skin, and four arms and sharp needle teeth which it snapped at Zevyn's head.

"It's a Tsist!" Iris widened her eyes. The Tsist flung Zevyn away, who landed on her feet. She glared up at the creature, but its attention was fixed on Iris.

"Avaron's daughter, aren't you?" It clacked its teeth. She nodded confidently. The Tsist's expression changed immediately. "Finally, you returned! Where are the others?"

Iris looked away. "We had to leave them behind," Ruben

explained. The Tsist's brown eyes widened. "Well, you can explain later," he said, but disbelief was evident in his voice. "My name is Dejkis. Call me Dej. I'll take you to Avaron." He turned around and vanished.

Dej led them to a huge clearing, which was packed with creatures of all kinds. Small settlements had been established in one side, while a training arena was made in another corner. Many were training, while some were moving out of the clearing.

Dej took them to the training area. Iris gasped as she noticed a familiar figure.

"Father!" she cried. Avaron turned sharply, and his opponent beat him. Avaron pushed him off and rushed to his daughter, a beaming smile on his face.

His initial enthusiasm faded when he saw only Lyke, Zevyn and Ruben with his daughter. He frowned. "Where are the others? And where is the lotus?"

Iris handed over the lotus to her father, but didn't answer his first question.

"Where are the others?" He repeated. Iris looked away, unable to meet her father's brilliant green gaze.

It was Ruben who answered. "The Lotus Guardian did not let us go. Ron distracted it and we managed to escape. They are still with that monster." he spat. Avaron didn't comment.

"What is your plan? When is the battle?" Lyke asked.

Avaron looked around at the cluster of various creatures and sighed.

"The battle is on the Night of Faztex. I will take you to the other leaders, they will tell you about the battle." He turned around and walked away, glancing back once. Iris followed her father with Ruben right behind her, and after a moment's hesitation, Lyke and Zevyn followed.

Avaron led them to a little crowded tent and ducked inside. They entered, and realized that all eyes were on them. Lyke shifted uncomfortably, pushing his much more confident sister in front of him.

Iris pushed past the siblings and joined her father at a table. Zevyn, Lyke and Ruben sat next to Iris and Avaron.

"Do you have the lotus?" A Streo asked them as soon as they sat down.

"Yes, Miva, they brought it," Avaron replied for them, handing over the lotus to the Streo. She inspected it, turning it over in her hands. After a moment of silence, she turned to the children.

"Well done, all of you. I, actually all of us doubted you, but you have proven that you are much more than capable of completing dangerous tasks." She smiled at them.

"But Avarron sssaid there were more off you," a Xasfi said, looking at them intently from clear green eyes.

"Yes, Storin, but the Lotus Guardian did not let them leave, they distracted it, and Iris, Ruben, Lyke and Zevyn escaped."

"So the rest of them are still stuck on Earth?"

Avaron nodded, sighing. The leaders exchanged worried glances.

"The Lotus Guardian is said to be very selfish. I guess it is not such a surprise that it used them to its own personal interests," the Veria leader said.

Iris shook her head. "We have to get them back," she argued.

"Yeah, we have to save them. Ron's father and Carra's mother too," Lyke agreed.

"Of course we will save them. But we cannot spare time before the battle. And if we lose against the Shadow, they will be better off on Earth," Avaron muttered darkly.

"We will *not* lose. We will defeat the Shadow of Death and destroy him once for all," Miva declared firmly. Everyone looked away, as if Miva's words didn't hit as close to home as she had expected.

"So what is the plan?" Zevyn asked finally.

Chapter 20

"Today is the day we will fight the Shadow! We will take back what was rightfully ours!" Avaron cried.

It was the day of the Night of Faztex. Everyone had assembled after one last time of training. The non-warriors of each tribe were also busy, making dummy warriors, sharpening blades, preparing last minute medicines for the healers.

"Chester, Scythor," Avaron said, addressing his bond and the Musker leader. "The tunnels are safe?" The lion and the Musker nodded.

"Good. Are the dummies ready?"

"Yes. We have to only place them for the battle."

"Well done. For victory!" he screamed. Everyone chorused, "For victory!"

"What about us, Father?" Iris asked, approaching Avaron after his speech.

"Hmm?" He looked at his daughter, tension apparent on his face.

"What are we going to do during the fight?" Iris asked again, glancing at her bond, Zevyn and Lyke.

"You four will be responsible for rescuing the Ronens while we distract The Shadow of Death. You will stay together and bring everyone to this clearing. No Ronen will be expected to fight. They will be treated and fed here, and you will *not* leave their side, understood?" Avaron looked sternly at Lyke, who nodded, subdued. “Okay, good.” With that, the Ronen leader left with Romial. Chester touched Iris’ shoulder with his tail in a friendly farewell, and padded after his bond.

“Are you ready?” Iris asked. “Hell, yeah.” Zevyn said, smiling slyly. Lyke just nodded, still feeling disappointed that he would not be participating in the battle. Ruben let out a loud screech, then laughed. “Of course I am ready!”

Iris shot her bond a warm glance, then shook her head and hugged him.

“Let’s do this.” Zevyn spread out her wings and soared upwards. Lyke frowned up at his sister. “We can’t all fly, you know.”

“Why are you so miserable?” she asked, landing next to her brother.

“I can’t fight in the battle,” he muttered grouchily.

“When we are rescuing the Ronens, we will encounter guards. The Shadow is not so stupid that he will leave his prisoners unguarded. We will leave all of them for you to practice your nonexistent battle skills,” Ruben laughed cheerfully. Lyke’s face brightened up considerably, not even seeming to have heard Ruben’s last sentence.

“Great!” Zevyn rolled her eyes. “Come on, battle lover.” Lyke, apparently pleased with his new nickname, followed his sister in high spirits. Ruben and Iris exchanged amused glances and trailed behind the siblings.

* * *

“How much longer?” Zevyn asked, fidgeting impatiently. Iris glanced exasperatedly at her. “Avaron will give the signal when everyone is ready,” she said, turning back to the scene in front of her. Iris, Zevyn and Lyke were crouched in the branches of trees, waiting for Avaron’s signal; the piercing screech of a Veria. Ruben was perched comfortably on a branch above their heads, preening himself.

Zevyn grumbled and tried to shift her position, but an ominous crack made her freeze. Her catlike eyes widened, but the screech of a Veria drowned out the sound of the branch breaking. The three of them tumbled to the ground, but Lyke was the only one who landed. Zevyn unfurled her wings and flew back to the tree, while Ruben saved his bond and carried her to safety. Fortunately though, Lyke fell right on top of a couple of the Shadow's minions who were passing by.

With a smile of grim satisfaction, Lyke successfully knocked both of them out. "All clear!" he called, looking up at his companions.

"Great," Iris smiled, landing nimbly on her feet. Zevyn swooped down, her face blank. Ruben remained in the air, looking around for danger.

"Three enemies from the west, two from north!" he called out. "I will handle those two, you take out the rest." With that, he flapped his wings and glided swiftly away. Iris, Zevyn and Lyke immediately faced west, and spotted the three henchmen.

With a loud cry, the three minions launched themselves in the air, and in a flash, one of them was on the ground, groaning in pain. Zevyn stood over him, her eyes glinting dangerously. A kick to his head silenced his cries. Behind her, Lyke had already dealt with both of them, the two bodies vibrating as electricity passed through them. He turned around to find Iris already jogging away, beckoning to them to join her.

A swoosh of wind signalled Ruben's arrival. "The coast is clear for now. The camp is completely overrun. We underestimated the Shadow's numbers. There are too many enemies left behind for us to handle," he stated plainly.

"Then we use stealth." Iris sounded determined. Zevyn nodded.

"What's the position?" Lyke asked. Ruben swooped up for a quick check, and landed beside them again.

"Two right in front. About three score in the camp. Two on the back and two on each side. The camp has been changed, *again*, and there is a huge pole in the middle. All the Ronens are chained to it."

"Why don't they just shift?" Zevyn asked curiously.

Iris shook her head. "Ronens have to be healthy to be able to shift. It is one of the downs of shifting."

"The Ronens have been tortured." Ruben shook his head. "There's no sign of any of the bonds."

"What?"

"I cannot see them."

"Those vermin have probably hidden them somewhere."

"So what's the plan?"

"You guys free the Ronens, I'll take out all the guards."

"Don't be stupid, Lyke. There are sixty guards in camp. There's no way you can take them all out, even with your lightning."

"But the element of surprise is the most important part in a battle," Lyke argued. "I can use lightning to knock out at least a quarter of them there, and they won't even know what hit them!"

"I agree, Lyke, but let one of us help you," Iris said patiently.

"Okay, okay," Lyke muttered. "Zevyn, you're up." His sister nodded. "Sure."

Lyke closed his eyes, summoning lightning from the skies.

"He could produce lightning on his own, could he not?" Ruben asked curiously. "His lightning is not powerful enough for mass scale destruction," Zevyn said, watching as her brother gathered storm clouds in the sky above. Soon, the air was crackling with the intensity of electricity. The Death Lord's minions were becoming unsettled and nervous, making them irritable. In a moment, a fight had already broken out between the soldiers.

Lyke turned to his friends, gave a beaming smile, and drew lightning from the stormy skies. Once it touched his hands, he lit up and rose a few feet above the ground. Opening his eyes determinedly, he sent the lightning surging towards the Ronen camp, controlling the bolts with his mind. Zevyn launched herself into the air the same instant, her wings sending strong gusts of wind in every direction.

The enemy soldiers scattered in every direction, completely forgetting their training. Lyke's lightning zapped out two dozen sentries, while Zevyn's wind blew away at least one score. The rest fled, but suddenly seemed to regain control and positioned themselves in a tactical battle formation.

Zevyn cursed. "What's wrong?" Lyke called. Zevyn quickly ducked to avoid being hit by a shower of arrows before replying. "They have a stupid smart general! They are standing in between all the prisoners, so there's no way you can take them out without risking the Ronens' lives."

"Then we draw them to us." Lyke said, throwing a bolt of lightning straight at the pole. It made an ominous *clang* on impact, but the pole didn't melt, as Lyke had expected it to. Instead, the bolts got deflected, aiming straight at Lyke. Everyone ducked, including the guards, and Zevyn took her chance, barrelling into one of the guards, killing him instantly.

The Ronens, who were watching all the while, regained hope and started struggling against the chains around their wrists.

"The keys! The ugly one in front of Ivy has the keys!" a voice rang out. Zevyn turned to see it was Leif who had spoken. The girl nodded swiftly and dived towards the one Leif had mentioned. *He is obviously the General, or he wouldn't have been trusted with the keys*, Zevyn reasoned with herself, *which means that he commands all these stupid creatures.*

"Lyke!" she called, soaring upwards. Lyke ran into the clearing on thunderbolts, rising higher with each step he took. He nodded to his sister when they were parallel. They split up, and the General, obviously thinking Lyke was more dangerous, kept a look-out on the boy, sending some of his soldiers after Zevyn.

The winged girl led the soldiers into the nearby forest where she quickly disposed of them. Feigning injuries, she dragged herself out into the clearing, in full view of the General.

"Zevyn, get back!" She heard Lyke scream as the General chuckled evilly. But the boy did nothing to save her, knowing full well that it was only an act to buy time and get rid of more minions. The Ugly General ordered some soldiers to finish her off. Faking a look of terror, she waited until they were on her, then suddenly she kicked out with her wings, the force of it sending all of them flying. Moving quickly, she killed all of them. The Ugly General's face had turned from gleeful triumph to a growing horror. Zevyn faced him now, her eyes cold and daunting. When he was distracted, Lyke ran down on his lightning to stand right behind the General and with a swift kick, sent him sprawling, away from the Ronens.

Picking up the key from the General's pocket he tossed it into the air. In a second, it was in Ruben's grip, who was already flying towards Iris. The two immediately set on rescuing the Ronens, while Lyke and Zevyn finished off the rest of the soldiers.

"Where are the animals?" Ruben asked Ivy as soon as she was free. "Come with me, I will take you," she said and jogged as fast as her starving body allowed her to. She halted and stamped on a certain patch of earth, and it gave way, revealing an underground entrance.

"When did they do this?" Zevyn asked, standing behind Ruben. "They have not been idle ever since they seized the camp."

"Okay, I'm going in," Zevyn said and ran down the flight of stairs. Iris immediately followed, but not without giving her sister a small hug first. It was very smelly in the underground cellar. Pretty soon, they found row upon row of cages, inside which all the animals had been locked up. Setting to work immediately, Zevyn had already opened two cages with her cat claws before realizing that Iris was still standing where she had left her.

"What's the matter?" "I cannot see like you, Zevyn. Have you forgotten?" Iris replied, raising an eyebrow. "Oh, here," Zevyn handed her friend a wooden torch she found. "How do I light it?" Iris asked, touching the torch. Zevyn sighed, and asked one of the free animals to fetch Lykenzar.

The boy came down and lit up the torch. Iris started to free the bonds with the key, while Zevyn resumed using her claws. After a few minutes of unlocking, all the animals were in the light once again.

"Where is the battle taking place?" Leif demanded once the last of the animals were out. "Umm, we're supposed to be taking you to the clearing, and then we're supposed to watch you guys. Avaron especially told us not to get involved in the battle." Lyke shrugged.

"We will eat, then those who are willing will help Avaron. We will not let our leader fight alone. It is a promise we made the moment we were born." Leif announced. A cheer from all the Ronens proved that the whole Clan agreed.

"I am not letting my husband fight alone." Iris' mother.

"This is not only Father's battle, it is all of ours." Ivy.

"I am not a coward. I will lay my life for my Clan."

"Avaron may need us. We cannot desert them at a time of need."

As more voices joined, Lyke sighed and turned to Zevyn. "Looks like we can't follow Avaron's order after all." Zevyn nodded glumly.

"Come on. We will take you to the clearing. Have some food and arm yourselves."

"Are we ready?" Leif's voice echoed around the clearing. A chorus of agreement satisfied him, and he turned around to face Iris and Ivy.

"Let us go."

Iris, Zevyn, Lyke and Ruben led the strongest Ronens to the clearing. They heard the sounds of battle long before they reached. The screeches of the Veria made the roars of Makix and the growls of the Musker sound as insignificant as a background drone, and the shouts and screams of the Streos, Hikints and the Shadow's army were barely heard at all.

"What is the plan?"

The Ronens gathered around Lyke, Zevyn, Iris and Ruben as they explained the leaders' plan.

Zevyn started sketching a diagram on the earth with her claws. "This is the main tunnel built by Chester and the Musker. It connects to these tunnels. The Musker would be hiding here, and when the Shadow comes, they collapse these two tunnels, so some of the Shadow's army go down. They put dummies all around here, so the Shadow will think we will attack from behind when in fact, we attack from the front itself."

"Double bluff. Nice," Leif commented.

"The Streo archers are here, on the Veria. They attack from up, and at the same time, this tunnel is collapsed."

"Attacked from up and down." Ivy couldn't help murmuring.

"Yeah. Then all around here, the Xasfi drag some soldiers into the forest and leave them there for the Tsist to take care of. The Xasfi go this bit, and with the Makix, separate a few soldiers to use for the catapult."

At this, Ivy started laughing. "Excellent idea!"

Lyke nodded. "The Hikints control the catapults. The Makix tie up the soldiers and give them to the Hikints, and they are catapulted onto their own army."

"Brilliant."

"After that, all of them regroup and attack the Shadow's army together. And right now, it sounds as though the Shadow's army is too big to have weakened them enough."

"So what are we waiting for?"

"We have to find out which stage of the plan they are in." Iris nodded.

"I can go," a tabby cat offered, padding up to Leif.

"Yes, thank you, Jaquar" Leif said. Jaquar slunk towards the battle field silently, sniffing the air every now and then. He disappeared behind a clump of ferns. After some time of impatient waiting, the cat reappeared at a run.

"They are all fighting already. The Shadow's army is too large for Avaron," he reported.

"Come on then. Let's save Imagneus!" Lyke cried, lightning appearing in his hands. He turned and ran for the battlefield with everyone behind him.

They spilled out onto the bloody field. They immediately saw that Jaquar was correct, the Shadow of Death's army outnumbered Avaron's three to one.

Lyke and Zevyn were the first to reach the battling armies. Their arrival caused the enemy army to stop in surprise, and that one second hesitation led to some of their deaths. Avaron's army seemed to have regained their hope that they might win, and they fought harder.

Iris wielded a sword and charged at four soldiers overpowering a Xasfi. The two headed beast could do nothing against the soldiers, and just as one had raised its sword to kill the Xasfi, Iris ploughed her sword through it, and it fell to the ground with a look of utter shock on its face.

While the other three were regaining their composure, the Xasfi attacked, killing all three with one blow of its long tail. Muttering a thanks to Iris, he swivelled his heads towards three more soldiers heading in their direction. He knocked out two with his tail, while Iris dealt with the third. And they fought on like that, side by side.

Ruben had taken to the skies, joining the Veria. One of them was carrying two archers, as the second archer's mount had succumbed to injuries. Ruben allowed the archer to sit on his back instead, receiving a nod of gratitude from the Veria.

Ivy had changed into a tiger, and was fighting back to back with Victoria, her bond. Their claws were swift and accurate, and helped many soldiers to leave the world.

Lyke and Zevyn together had taken a tour of the battleground, yet could not find the Death Lord anywhere.

"The coward! He is making his soldiers fight his battles while he slinks around, out of harm's way!" Zevyn spat.

"We'd better not waste time. Come on," Lyke said, jumping down on his thunderbolts. When he was near the ground, he started showering lightning onto the Shadow's enemies, who screamed in terror, but did not flee. Zevyn joined her brother, swooping low to distract the soldiers while Lyke killed them.

And the fight wore on, the sun set, and the moons rose to glory. Faztex shone brighter than the others, and suddenly dark clouds covered the sky. Avaron's army fought on, undeterred, but unsettled when their enemies started grinning wickedly.

"What in the world?" Lyke whispered, staring as the clouds formed a giant face.

"It's the Death Lord!" Zevyn gasped.

Something in Lyke's head seemed to click, and he immediately formed a lightning shield, attempting to protect the whole battleground, but he wasn't powerful enough. He could shield only half the ground, not more. Zevyn rose until she was level with the clouds and tried to blow the clouds away, using her wings to create tremendous winds, but even that didn't work. The clouds started pouring, but what came down wasn't rainwater, it was decaying bits of flesh, which on making contact with the ground, turned into horrifying lifelike replicas of everyone still breathing in Avaron's army.

They started marching slowly, staggering like zombies. The Death Lord's laughter wafted from the clouds.

"How are we going to defeat them?" A Hikint whispered, terrified. All the creatures backed away, forming a frightened group in one side of the field. An evil Veria flapped its wings, but they were torn and it couldn't use them.

An idea flashed into Avaron's head. "That is how! They cannot fly!" he gasped. The others seemed to have realized it too, and every creature which could fly spread their wings, but all of a sudden, the Death lord made a face in the clouds, and it flashed to everyone that if they flew up, the Shadow would destroy them for sure.

Lyke helplessly struck his own evil twin with lightning, and to his surprise, it disintegrated and an even more unpleasant reek filled the air.

"Their weakness is lightning? Or is it the elements?" Lyke wondered out loud. Zevyn's eyes flashed with hope. She immediately flew towards one of the Veria and asked her to spit fire at the zombies. The Veria did as she asked and as soon as the flames touched some evil Makix, they screamed and turned to ashes.

Avaron laughed. "Genius!"

All the Veria assembled in front of everyone else at once and rained fire on the zombies. In no time, everything was ashes. A furious roar stopped them in their tracks and the Shadow descended onto the ground. His soldiers immediately positioned themselves behind their Lord.

The Shadow of Death opened his mouth in a soundless scream and the clouds fell to the ground. Lyke immediately put up his lightning shield, and the clouds were electrified and turned to smoke as soon as they touched it. As soon as the last cloud was gone Lyke sat on the ground, his energy drained.

Avaron stepped forward. "You fight me, one on one," he challenged the Shadow, who only smiled wickedly. The Death Lord launched himself at Avaron without a warning, but the Ronen leader was ready. Just before the Shadow of Death reached him, he held out the little crystal lotus, and the Shadow crashed into the lotus instead of Avaron. The lotus went straight through the Death lord's chest and embedded itself there. With a startled cry, he glanced down at the transparent lotus sitting in his chest, growing bigger and bigger, spreading throughout his body.

"What have you done?" he whispered at Avaron, falling down, trying to pull out the lotus. The crystal flower grew and grew until it filled his whole body, and he turned into crystal too, before breaking into a million pieces. Only one small part was intact, in the shape of a little lotus.

Chapter 21

Everyone stared in shock for a few moments. Then Lyke shouted, "It's over!" and suddenly everyone was screaming in ecstasy.

"We did it!" Ruben flew to his bond. Ivy changed back to normal and hugged Victoria. Avaron was still staring at the crystal pieces in front of him, as if he still couldn't believe it was over.

The Shadow's minions stared at what was once their leader. Realization that they were leaderless hit them like a brick. As one, they turned and fled, climbing over each other to escape. The Veria and Tsists finished them, taking no prisoners.

Everybody made a huge deal out of going back to the clearing; dancing and singing the whole way. They shared the wonderful news with the joyful non-warriors of the clans and tribes, who went out of their way to create a tremendous feast for dinner for the starving battlers.

After eating like never before, they were quickly treated before partying the rest of the night. A peaceful noon greeted them was they woke, and they were reminded of the task in front of them; paying tribute to the fallen.

They went to the battleground and carried all the dead back to the clearing, where they were cleaned up and ready to be buried. It was a solemn procession that took the bodies to their final resting place. A teary farewell followed the digging of many graves, mostly done by the Musker again.

When the sorrowful job was completed, they gathered in the clearing again, where Iris reminded her father of May, Ron, Carra and Josh.

"We shall fetch the other children now itself," he decided. Calling Minkin, the two discussed the matter with Avaron's wife. By evening, Minkin had opened a doorway straight into the Lotus Guardian's lair. Avaron himself went through, with Ivy and Leif. Iris, Ruben, Lyke and Zevyn decided to stay back, not willing to meet the serpent again.

In no time, Avaron was back with all of them, and Jessica and Josh's father too, whom Avaron had picked up from his home.

A happy reunion took place, and introductions were made, and the Ronens finally set off, back to their camp.